Deadly Surprise

The Early Bird Café Cozy Mystery Series

by Ginny Gold

CONTENTS

CHAPTER 1

Kori was nervous beyond belief. She couldn't believe she'd said yes. She was going on a date with Zach Gulch. After nearly twenty years of pretending she didn't have feelings for him, here she was getting all dolled up and was as jumpy as a teenager.

"Where is he taking you?" Nora asked, seated on Kori's bed. Kori knew she wouldn't be able to make all the important decisions about what to wear and how to do her hair so she'd asked her best friend to come over.

"Jackson's," Kori said, turning around to gauge Nora's reaction. Jackson's was located on the north side of Thrush Lake, looking south toward Hermit Cove. The outside seating was perfectly located so they would be able to look back at their hometown while they enjoyed the fanciest meal in the state.

"I can't believe he could get a table so fast!" Nora reacted exactly how Kori knew she would—shouting in excitement and leaping off the bed. Kori blushed and turned back to the mirror to work on her makeup.

"Let me do that," Nora said, coming up beside her and taking the mascara from her hand. "You're shaking and you're just going to smudge it."

It was true. Kori gladly let Nora take over. They were celebrating the two month anniversary of Kori clearing her name and solving the first murder case in Hermit Cove in decades and she wanted to look her best.

"Have you decided what you're going to wear?" Kori was still wrapped in a towel, a second one on her head drying her hair.

"No. That's why you're here," Kori joked, but she was dead serious.

"Well, let's think about this. It's late May so it could still be cold at night. What time is your reservation?"

"Seven. He's picking me up in half an hour," Kori said as calmly as she could while her heart beat against her ribs at the thought of how soon she'd be with Zach.

"You'll want something that will keep you warm enough. I'm almost done with your makeup and then we're going to raid your closet."

Nora put the finishing touches on Kori's face and then stepped back to admire her work. "Look in the mirror," Nora instructed her. "What do you think?"

"You do amazing work." Kori couldn't take her eyes off herself. She wasn't usually vain, but she looked great. Her eyes popped and the color on her cheeks wasn't overdone.

"Now, to the closet!" Nora wasted no time with dawdling. She took off as if she were headed for the Batcave.

Inside Kori's closet they start rifling through the few dresses Kori had acquired over the years. She had the dress she'd worn to a friend's wedding in New York years ago, but it was strapless and wouldn't work in this weather. There was the dress she'd bought for almost nothing at a consignment shop just before a vacation to the beach. But it wasn't formal enough for this evening.

"This is it," Nora said, pulling a fitted maroon dress from its hanger. Kori'd had it altered years ago and had never had a reason to wear it. Until now. A friend, who was a bit heftier than Kori's size six, had given it to her. After paying pennies to have it adjusted, it fit her perfectly.

"But it has no sleeves. And it doesn't come past my knees. I'll be cold," Kori protested.

"You have a white sweater?" Nora asked, checking what else was in the closet. She pulled a cashmere cardigan off a hanger. "Here, put this on too."

Kori took the towel off of her head and let her wet hair fall down her back. She knew Nora wouldn't let her get away with her usual ponytail tonight. She slipped the dress over her head and let it slide down her body and at the same time she let the towel fall away.

"Zip?" Kori asked and turned around so Nora could zip the back.

"Perfect," Nora said, admiring Kori. "Sit on the bed. I'll do your hair."

Kori paused in front of the mirror and took in her new look. Her chest had never been her proudest feature, but the tightness of the dress accentuated it just enough to make her take a second glance. And the underwire bra did miracles. She was glad she'd decided to take the time to shave her legs.

Finally, Kori did as instructed and sat on her bed. She wondered where Nora got her fashion sense since farming required her to usually dress in baggy overalls and boots but she loved that her best friend complemented her own complete lack of any desire to be fashionable.

Nora plugged in the hair dryer and got to work. They were running out of time. She combed while she dried and ended up with perfectly straight, flowing blonde hair. A side part let some hair fall in front of Kori's face, making her even more enticing.

As soon as the hair dryer was turned off, the doorbell rang and Kori gave Nora a look of fear. "Don't worry. This is *Zach*," Nora reminded her. "You've known him your whole life."

Kori nodded. "Right. I'll get the door. Let yourself out after we leave."

"Have such a great time." Nora hugged Kori and started cleaning up the makeup and hair accessories. "Remember, let him treat you like the princess you are."

Kori slipped on her sandals—she could only hope that they matched her dress since they hadn't had time to work through that piece of her outfit—and headed quickly downstairs through The Early Bird Café and opened the front door. In front of her was heart stopping Zach Gulch, childhood crush she'd always thought was out of her league.

"Wow," he said, eyes growing wide with lust. She watched his smile spread and she returned it with one of her own. "Not only am I finally taking Kori Cooke out to dinner, but she looks . . . beautiful."

Kori smiled and looked at her feet quickly. "You look great, too," she said shyly, looking back up into Zach's eyes. Those eyes. She couldn't get enough of them. They were swimming pool blue and made her think of summer.

"Ready to go?" he asked and offered his arm.

Kori gladly accepted and walked to his car.

***

Once Zach and Kori were seated at their table at Jackson's—right on the water—Kori's nerves picked up again. She'd relaxed in the car with the radio to distract her but now that it was just the two of them, her words seemed to have sunk to the bottom of the lake.

"Business picking up for the summer?" Zach asked, seemingly unaware of her inability to make conversation.

"It is. And it doesn't hurt that The Early Bird is the only café in town again." She could have kicked herself under the table at bringing up her rival's murder.

Zach just chuckled. "I'm sure it doesn't. Something to drink?" he asked, picking up the drink menu and looking it over. "A bottle of wine?"

"That'd be great."

"Red or white?"

"Red."

"Are you cold?" he asked, concern in his voice.

Kori shook her head. She was actually sweating from the adrenaline coursing through her veins but shivering at the same time from nervousness. She couldn't figure out why she couldn't reel in her nerves. She'd known Zach her whole life, what was wrong with her tonight?

The waiter came to their table and Zach ordered a bottle of red wine and a fried calamari appetizer. Kori wondered, *How is he so calm?*

"How's work going for you?" she finally asked when the waiter had walked away. *Really? Work?* She chided herself for being so lame.

Zach didn't seem to care. "Quiet since Tessa's murder. Now it's back to DUIs and speeding tickets."

"That's a good thing, right?" Kori asked.

"Yes. We don't need another murder in Hermit Cove."

They were interrupted again with the wine arriving. Zach tasted it and approved the bottle before both of their glasses were filled.

Zach held up his glass and Kori mirrored him. "To a quiet future," he said and their glasses clinked together gently. She quickly wondered if he meant the future in general or theirs specifically. That thought made her smile.

The first sip immediately calmed Kori and she started to enjoy herself more, letting herself admire Zach for the person he was—down to earth, kind and always ready to give a hand to someone in need.

"Hey, have you hired another detective since Gunn was arrested?"

"Yup. Just yesterday. Detective Lani Silver."

"A girl?" Kori wasn't sure why she was surprised.

Zach nodded in confirmation and then changed the subject. "Tell me about your life in New York City." Kori easily slipped into stories from the years she lived away from Hermit Cove and started to thoroughly enjoy the evening.

She told stories and watched his body respond to her words. His blue eyes sparkled when he laughed; his broad shoulders relaxed more with each story; his short hair reflected the setting sun, giving it a tinge of red. Her heart was racing faster and faster as she looked at his muscular body.

She finally understood why she'd been so nervous—she desperately wanted this relationship to work.

***

Zach pulled up to the Early Bird Café just after ten that night. Kori sat in the passenger seat longer than she'd intended hoping the night wouldn't end.

"Tonight was, well—" Kori looked at Zach, temporarily speechless. She tried again. "I had an awesome time tonight," she told him, her nerves totally gone after the hours they'd spent together chatting about everything.

"Me too." Zach returned her gaze and put his arm around Kori.

"Thanks for taking me out. I can't even think of the last time I went out to dinner."

"It was my pleasure. We could do it again if you wanted."

Kori smiled and leaned slightly toward Zach. He met her halfway and they kissed for the first time after years of avoiding their true feelings. She had imagined this kiss many times but the real thing was so much better.

"Good night, Zach," Kori said, slightly speechless.

"Good night, Kori."

Kori let herself out of the car and into her café. She couldn't remember walking upstairs but somehow she made it to her living room. She sat on the couch, turned the TV on and relived the last several hours. Her eyes were unseeing but the sound of whatever show was on was a welcome sound. Eventually she headed to the bathroom to wash her face free of the makeup Nora had so expertly applied and brush her teeth before going to bed.

At four the next morning her alarm rang and Kori slowly opened her eyes. She was still on a high from her date and knew that today would be a good day.

It was Sunday, often the busiest day for her. She pulled on a pair of jeans and a black t-shirt and headed downstairs to get everything ready.

She started with the coffee. She didn't offer anything fancy, just a variety of roasts including coffee from Kona, Hawaii—a personal favorite—Tanzania, Ethiopia and Guatemala. She added additional varieties sometimes, depending on what was available in bulk and for what price. She had large pots that customers could order on the go, or if they were staying for a meal she ground fresh beans and served them in a French press.

Today she would make Kona and Ethiopian in the large pots and she got them going right away.

Then she headed to the walk-in freezer and fridge. Yesterday before she'd left for the day she'd made squash and sage biscuit dough. She took that out and set it on the counter. Everything else had been eaten and she'd have to make everything from scratch this morning.

Belgian waffles were easy, so those immediately went down as a menu option. She would make whipped cream that she would pair with strawberries. Or maple syrup.

She also had plenty of veggies from Nora's Red Clover Farm including kale and spinach, which were great additions to smoothies. Mixed with frozen fruit, yogurt and a little juice, green smoothies were a great Sunday morning breakfast side.

With granola, she'd add yogurt and fruit. And finally, she needed egg options. Feeling overly ambitious after last night, she considered popovers and huevos rancheros.

All of this went on the three chalkboard menus painted directly on the walls and then she set to work getting everything ready.

Fruits were placed next to the blender with yogurt, milk and juice nearby. Containers of granola, more yogurt and fruit were placed next to tall stemmed glasses that she'd serve them in. Waffle batter was whipped up and she placed that next to the waffle press, followed by whipped cream, strawberries and syrup. She made popover batter and took out her four popover pans. They had to bake for longer than anything else so she even stuck one pan in the preheated oven to get them started before she opened. And finally, she got gravy started and placed the first tray of biscuits in the oven as well.

Kori was feeling proud of her early morning energy when she glanced at the clock. It was already ten to six and she hadn't unlocked the door or flipped the sign to open! She'd never been so engrossed in her work that she'd forgotten to open on time at five thirty but there was a first for everything.

She quickly walked to the front of the café and opened the door. She was happy to see Jenna and Kyle Rhodes patiently waiting outside for her to open.

"Sorry for the delay," Kori told them as she held the door for them to enter.

"No worries. We didn't want to rush you so we walked up and down Main Street and enjoyed the quiet," Jenna told her. Then asked with a smile, "Late night last night?" Jenna winked and Kori blushed.

"No later than usual. I got so caught up in my cooking and getting everything ready that I didn't notice the time. Can I get you some coffee to start?"

Jenna and Kyle sat across from each other in a booth by the front windows with a view of Main Street.

"Black coffee for me. Kona," Jenna said, glancing at the menu to see what was available. Kyle held up two fingers to indicate he'd take the same.

Kori headed back to the kitchen and ground some beans, put them in a French press and poured hot water over them. She brought that to their table with two mugs.

"What are you putting in your smoothies?" Jenna asked when Kori set everything down on their table.

"There are plenty of options for you to choose from. I have kale or spinach for the greens, apple juice, orange juice or coconut water for the liquid, and bananas, strawberries, blueberries, blackberries, pineapple and mango for the fruits. And a yogurt base. Do you think you want one?"

"Not sure yet. Give us a couple more minutes," Jenna requested, looking at her husband and seeing that he was nowhere near knowing what he wanted.

"Sure." Kori turned and headed to the oven to check on the popovers and biscuits. Both were ready so she took them out and got seconds of both ready to be popped into the oven once more customers arrived.

The door opened just then and Kori looked up to see who had entered. A group of three adults came inside, looking slightly lost— tourists, she assumed—and Betsy Scoop was with Vera Joy, the owner of Furry Friends, the animal shelter across the street from The Early Bird. Kori didn't wait for anyone to order popovers or biscuits and gravy; she put the second trays of each in the oven and headed back out to make the rounds.

Kori started an easy conversation with Betsy and Vera, two people she had known for a long time. "Good morning. How's the move for Scoop's Scoops going?" she asked Betsy who looked up and smiled.

"All moved in! Can you believe how late I'm opening? I can't believe it took almost two months since the whole disaster with Tessa for things to get finalized," Betsy told her, visibly more relaxed now that she'd be able to open her business

Two months ago, Hermit Cove had seen its first murder in years— something that everyone was worried would put a damper on the summer tourist season. Tessa Doyle, the owner of a second café, had been murdered and Kori had been the prime suspect given their unfriendly past as students and near colleagues in New York City. Instead of landing in jail, Kori had cracked the case and Betsy had been able to move her ice cream shop, Scoop's Scoops, into the larger area that had been occupied briefly by the café.

"That's great to hear. Are you opening today?"

"I am. I can't wait. I have two high school sophomores working for me and I'm so excited to be able to expand so much this year."

"Congratulations!" Kori said with genuine excitement. She was happy for her friend and also for Hermit Cove's growing popularity. "And how are the cats and dogs?" she asked, turning to Vera.

"I was hoping you'd ask. I just got the perfect dog for you—she's four, so a little older, but friends with everyone. It was an owner surrender. I know you keep saying you're not ready, but I'm telling you, this dog is for you."

Kori looked down at her feet. She wanted to adopt a dog so badly but had been putting it off because she worked such long days and didn't want to leave a pet home alone all day. She didn't think that was fair to the animal.

"And the best part is that she used to go to a retirement home as a casual therapy dog, so you know she'd be fine in the café with customers." Vera's face was full of hope.

"I'll think about it," Kori finally managed. And she would. "What can I get you started with?"

The rest of the morning proved as busy as it started with the wait getting as long as twenty minutes. Kori knew she was almost in Betsy's position of needing to hire help—at least for the summer—and possibly even expand. The café only seated twenty people, so she could usually keep up with the rush. But if she didn't have to, why was she still pushing herself?

Midway to lunch, Kori's heart started fluttering when she saw Zach Gulch walk in with who she assumed was his new detective, Lani Silver. She tried to study her from afar and was disappointed to see that she was gorgeous: at least six feet tall, soft features that were easy to look at and a smile that got men turning their heads away from their breakfasts. *Could Zach possibly be attracted to her? Had he hired her because she would be nice to look at every day?*

They took a seat at the counter in front of the window where she worked and Kori was suddenly speechless.

"Morning Kori. I thought I'd give Detective Silver the grand tour of Hermit Cove this morning and we're finishing up here."

Kori managed to croak out a reply, "You're already finished? It's not even noon yet. There's got to be more to see in Hermit Cove."

"Well, we stopped by Red Clover Farm, Furry Friends, the market, the rec center, the auto body, post office and school—even though they were closed for Sunday—and now we're here." Zach's smile this morning had the same reaction in Kori's knees as it'd had last night. Only this time she was standing so had to look away before they buckled right beneath her. *But was the smile only for her or was part of it reserved for the amount of time he was going to be spending with Detective Silver?*

"Welcome to Hermit Cove," Kori managed to sputter to her new competition for Zach's heart. She tried to keep her voice calm and friendly but wasn't sure she'd managed completely. "Can I get you both something? On the house. As a welcome-to-Hermit-Cove gift," she added quickly, not wanting Lani to think that she always treated Zach that way. Or maybe she should let her think that; make sure she knew he was off limits. But was he? Had she really staked enough claim after just one date?

"I'll take one of the smoothies," Zach said. "Thanks."

There was that smile again that left Kori's knees weak and her heart skipping a couple of beats.

"Thanks Kori. Just a coffee. Black," Lani ordered.

Kori was relieved and disappointed that she couldn't stay to chat with Lani, but especially with Zach. Last night had been such an eye opener for her that she wanted it to continue right away but she also wanted to be sure that she was going down a path she was ready for. She wasn't quite sure how to balance those two emotions—and keep Lani at bay if there was any interest there.

At one, Kori finally sat down. She didn't even have the energy to close and lock the door first but everyone in town knew she was closed. It was only tourists she'd have the chance of having to turn away.

Suddenly the door opened. She looked up from the discarded newspaper she was reading, ready to apologize to whoever had entered, and saw her brother's worried face. "What is it?" she asked.

"It's Heidi. She's dead."

CHAPTER 2

"Heidi? Who's Heidi?" Kori asked, confused and not yet panicked.

"Heidi Fischer." Jay was breathing hard and the look of fear on his face hadn't diminished at all.

Kori waited for him to continue, still not understanding his concern.

Jay sat across from her in the booth and told her more. "Heidi Fischer," he repeated to no avail. "Remember how I told you I was using online dating websites?" Kori nodded. "She was the first woman I contacted. And she was killed yesterday morning."

"Oh." Kori was speechless. She wasn't sure if Jay had continued having a relationship with her from his initial contact, or when that even was, and wasn't sure how she should react. "How did you find out?" She knew it was a stupid question but couldn't stop herself from asking.

"Facebook."

"Facebook?"

"Yeah. We were Facebook friends. I didn't think anything of it when she requested to be my friend years ago. We didn't keep in touch. But I guess when everyone started posting on her wall—things that she won't ever see—it made it on to my news feed."

"That's bizarre."

Jay nodded.

"So someone you used to date is dead—"

"Let's just be clear about one thing: we never actually dated," Jay interrupted her, his hands moving wildly to further make his point.

"Okay. Someone you used to—what? Online date? What's the proper term?" Kori asked, trying to be more sensitive but still unsure of why Jay felt like he was in trouble.

"I don't even know. I never saw her either. Sure, we online dated."

"So someone you used to *online date* is dead. Killed. But what does this have to do with you?" she asked.

"From what's been posted on Facebook, it was someone she had met through the dating site we both used. The dating website keeps getting thrown around like they didn't do a proper vetting process for their users. I don't know how many people she online dated—or dated—through there, but I know I'm one of them."

"But that seems like a long shot. Where did she even live?"

"Not far. Scoter Circle."

"And you never met her?" Scoter Circle was only an hour away so it would have been plenty easy for Jay to have met Heidi if there had been anything in their online relationship to build upon.

"I know. She was the first person I contacted online so I wanted to see how that worked first," Jay said, clearly defending himself.

"Okay, well I won't be like Mom and give you a hard time about your relationship choices. But I don't really know why you're worried. Check out her online profile—if it's still up—and calm down. You know you didn't do it." Kori didn't add the final word she'd wanted to—*right?*

"I know. I just panicked and knew you'd understand."

"What, because I was a suspect in a murder case?"

Jay looked at her sheepishly and nodded.

"I'm here for you if that happens, don't worry. I've gotta get things cleaned up. You eat lunch yet?"

Jay shook his head and followed Kori into the kitchen. There, she looked through what was left and whipped up huevos rancheros for both of them. Then they sat back down in the same booth.

"How's Mom lately?" Jay asked after he'd taken a few bites in silence. Kori wasn't sure if he was still worrying about Heidi or if he was actually starving.

"Good. I haven't seen her this weekend. She usually comes in Monday before her spin class so I'll see her tomorrow morning."

"Oh, she actually told me she was gonna be out of town for the weekend. You'll never guess where she was going." Jay put his fork down noisily and the fear returned to his face. Kori waited. "Scoter Circle."

Kori refused to believe that her mother's visit to Scoter Circle could possibly be connected to Heidi Fischer's murder. "I have to assume that she never met Heidi so didn't even know she existed."

Jay nodded.

"So you're just putting two completely unrelated people and events together and thinking they are suddenly connected."

Jay nodded again. "I know. It's ridiculous. I just can't stop thinking that I might be a suspect."

"Well, stop thinking that. Because you just might make it come true."

***

After Jay left, Kori got to work cleaning up the kitchen. Since she wasn't swamped with other things to do, she decided to get the menu ready for Monday and maybe even give herself an extra ten minutes of sleep in the morning.

The smoothies had been a huge hit so she knew she'd have to start offering them regularly and she left them on the menu. She checked on the leafy greens she used and saw that she had to restock her kale supply. She started a list that she would take to Nora's as soon as she was finished with the menu.

Next, she added breakfast casserole. She'd make two—one vegetarian and one with bacon. She knew the bacon one would sell faster, and completely, but there were always plenty of vegetarians who wanted something eggy.

She hadn't made bread in quite a while, so she paused in her menu planning to get a batch of dough going. She always made enough for two loaves and they sold out every time. A thick piece of toast loaded with butter and jam or honey was one of the best starts to the day she thought.

It only took her a few minutes to get the ingredients weighed and laid out to add to the bowl in increments. She started with the warm water and dough, mixing it by hand just until it was combined. Then she had to let it rest before adding the salt and yeast. She kept her bread simple and baked it in Dutch ovens so they had nice crisp crusts and soft fluffy centers.

Kori always had at least one option of waffles, French toast or pancakes—something to cure the morning sweet tooth. So she added cinnamon French toast and banana or plain pancakes, they started with the same batter and she just added bananas later to those specific orders. She found that fruity pancakes sold much better than plain ones but it was easy enough to offer both. And she always had too-old bananas around that needed to be used.

When she had the menu completely planned, she returned to her bread and added the rest of the ingredients, folding them in until everything was combined. She set it aside, ran upstairs to change her shirt and came back in time to fold it again and let it rise. She knew she had a few hours before she'd have to separate the dough into the two loaves and stick them in the fridge overnight, so she headed outside to her car to refill her vegetable and egg supplies from Red Clover Farm.

"Hey Kori," Nora said, standing up from her kneeling position next to one of her raised beds. "I thought you might stop by this afternoon."

"I couldn't wait for tomorrow morning's egg delivery. There was other stuff I needed so thought I'd come by. How's your weekend?"

"Boring. Tell me about *yours*. How did the date go? I can't believe you made me wait all day to hear the details and didn't call as soon as you got home."

"It was late," Kori said lamely and Nora rolled her eyes. "But it was so great." Kori couldn't hold in her excitement anymore. She let out all of the details of what she loved about the evening—how special she felt getting dressed up; how every time she got Zach to laugh she got butterflies in her stomach; how his deep blue eyes never got old looking at across the table; how she was constantly reminded of growing up alongside him and wasting all those years they weren't together.

"I don't want to say it, but I told you so!" Nora said, showing as much excitement as Kori was feeling. "You guys are perfect for each other. When's the next date?"

"We didn't make plans," Kori realized with regret. "But I saw him today at The Early Bird. And his new detective, Lani Silver, is a bombshell. Either he stopped by because he wanted to see me or because he wanted to show me that I had competition."

"Oh please. That man hasn't stopped loving you since high school. You think that some out of town beauty can steal his heart? Are you kidding me? You're the one I had to convince to go out with him, not Zach. He's been waiting for that day for more than half his life. There's no way you have competition."

Kori felt only a little reassured. "Yeah right. You think he was always obsessed with me but he's dated plenty."

"That was just to fill the time until you came to your senses. Now that you've finally done that, no one is going to get him to turn his head."

"Okay. Whatever. I'm here on business you know," Kori teased.

"Sure. What do you need?"

Kori followed Nora to the kale and spinach that had been growing outside for over a month and they started picking the best leaves and putting them in a box.

"Vera stopped by today," Nora said, both women hunched over and sifting through the greens.

Kori wasn't surprised. "Oh yeah? What'd she want?"

"She told me about a retired service dog that just came in. Owner surrender."

"That's not quite what she told me."

Nora looked up and smiled. "I should have known she'd come to you first. What was her story then?"

"She wasn't a therapy dog but used to go to retirement homes unofficially."

"Okay, I might have embellished that part. I just thought maybe you'd be ready for a four legged friend." Nora's eyes looked like those that Kori imagined the dog must have—pleading.

"What about you? Don't Milo and Otis need a young friend to keep them active?" Kori knew she was digging.

"Hah! Those dogs are more active than most four year old dogs! They'd be keeping her active I think. Besides, I promised myself I wouldn't get another one until they're gone," Nora whispered so the dogs wouldn't know what she meant.

"Fine. You guys are breaking me down. I'll go look at the dog on my way back to The Early Bird."

"Great! We knew you'd cave eventually. And it sounds like this is a dog worth caving for."

Kori knew her friends were right—she was ready for a dog. And from what Vera said, this would be the perfect dog to add to The Early Bird Café family.

"Now what about those eggs?" Kori asked, her box full of fresh greens overflowing in her arms.

"I'm so glad you got more chickens for me. I don't think I'd be able to keep up with the demand!"

Nora was now up to 32 hens, thanks to Kori buying 14 retired layers. They were only a couple years old so didn't produce quite as much as Nora's young birds, but they still had plenty of eggs left in them.

"Just let me know if you need more. It sounds like they're always looking for homes for the hens when they stop laying an egg a day."

"If they'd just give them a better environment they'd get more eggs out of them. I've been getting five eggs a week from some of the new girls. I think that's pretty good for a retired layer."

"You have different standards I think. I'm your only customer," Kori joked.

"Well, you do make it that way."

"Hey, what are you saying? That you'd like to sell elsewhere?" Kori was laughing.

"Nope. Just that you're good enough business to keep me out of eggs to sell anywhere else!"

Kori and Nora, followed by Milo and Otis, made their way to the chicken coop and started checking the nesting boxes. Then they headed to the barn where more eggs were waiting for them in the fridge. Altogether, there were eight dozen—enough for about half the week. And Kori knew she could always just plan her menu accordingly. But with the late May air, she also knew the chickens would soon be at their peak productivity.

"You have the farm stand open yet?" Kori asked once her arms were free and all of her fresh food was loaded into the car.

"Planned for this week. I'm really excited about it. Come by for the opening Wednesday night."

"Great. I'll see you then, if not sooner," Kori said, and jumped in her car.

She got back to The Early Bird, unloaded her produce into the walk-in fridge and, as promised, headed across the street to Furry Friends.

"I'm so glad you came!" Vera exclaimed before the door was even closed behind Kori.

Kori gave a sheepish smile. "I saw Nora," she said simply.

"I just know this will be the dog for you. Come."

Kori followed Vera obediently past cages of dogs. For a small town, Kori was always surprised how many dogs came and went through Furry Friends. They were mostly shipped north from states and cities that were overrun with mistreated pets and strays who were given a second chance in and around Hermit Cove.

"Here she is."

Kori stopped next to Vera and looked into the cage. She saw a short haired white dog with a few black markings. She was the only dog not adding to the racket, but instead was sitting patiently, confident that she'd soon be taken to her new home.

The dog looked up at Kori's face and turned her head to the side like she knew Vera was trying to send her home with this new person.

"Let me get a leash and you guys can meet outside."

Kori was unable to deny her this request. She wouldn't admit it but the dog had already won her over.

Vera led Kori to a small enclosed area outside and then left her alone to collect the dog. When she returned, the dog walked directly next to Vera, not pulling on the leash at all, and trotted straight to Kori.

"She came in with the name Bella but she doesn't seem to respond to it specifically," Vera explained.

Bella sat at Kori's side and looked up at her face. Kori couldn't keep her hand from stroking her head. "What kind is she?"

"A good old fashioned mutt. We think some shepherd. Maybe some pitt. But don't let that scare you off. Like I said, she used to regularly visit a retirement home."

"Why was she given up?" Kori asked, thinking there must be a dark spot in her past.

"No idea. Could have been an elderly person's pet and the kids didn't want to keep her. Or someone moved. Or they just didn't commit long term. Hard to say. But she's going to go fast. So I knew I had to get you in today to see her."

As Vera spoke, Kori squatted down to Bella's level and petted her more vigorously. Bella responded by nearly smiling.

"You guys are right—it's time I quit putting it off and adopt the dog I've been wanting."

"That's great. You'll take her home right now then?"

Kori looked up from Bella's face and nodded. "But I'm changing her name. She has the markings of an Ibis. That's what I'm going to call her."

"No problem. I can get you registered with the dog officer and everything right now. She's up to date on shots. I'll get all the paperwork for you."

Vera walked out of the kennel and back inside, leaving Kori with Ibis to bond. "What do you think?" Kori asked her new pet. "You think you'll be a good welcoming dog at The Early Bird? I had to give you a bird name if that's where you're going to work."

Ibis wagged her tail in response.

***

Kori brought Ibis home and then walked down Main Street to Hermit Market. This was the only place in town that she could think of where she'd be able to buy a dog bed and some food. As soon as she walked in the owner greeted her.

"Kori, it's been so long since you came in here," Teddi West said, a huge smile across his face. He was her mother's age and had been Kori's neighbor growing up. He'd always been a better male role model for her than her father had been. "Have you been shopping somewhere else?"

Kori gave Teddi a quick hug. "I've been getting all my produce from Nora now that the growing season is in full swing. And I've been buying in bulk direct from suppliers for the nonperishables I need." She was slightly embarrassed to have to admit that to Teddi, whose business she'd love to support more.

"We'll have to talk about that," he teased, mock betrayal in his voice. "I could try to get you deals too."

"Sure. We can do that." Kori was happy about the prospect of working with him. "But today I'm here for a dog bed and some dog food."

"You finally adopted a dog from Vera!" Apparently the whole town had been rooting for this day.

"I did." Kori nodded and smiled. She really was happy to be adding this dog to her family.

"Well, let's go see what I have."

Kori followed Teddi to the pet supply area and she picked out two beds—one for The Early Bird Café and one for her house above the café. She knew Ibis would likely be sleeping on the couch or her bed, but she'd try her best to confine her to her own dog bed.

Kori walked back up Main Street and was surprised to find Zach waiting at the café's front door, his back to her.

"Hi," she greeted him, excitement filling her at the sight of him— alone this time.

"Hey. Let me help you with those." Zach took the beds from Kori so she was left with just the bag of dog food. She placed it on the ground and unlocked the door. "You got a dog," he stated.

"Yup. Vera and Nora finally talked me into it. Come inside and meet her—Ibis."

They both maneuvered themselves upstairs and Kori found Ibis making herself at home on the couch. Kori and Zach laughed.

"These beds might be overkill. It looks like she already found where she wants to sleep," Zach said.

"Yup. I knew that was a possibility. I'm planning to bring her to The Early Bird with me. Don't worry, she'll stay in my office until she passes a good citizen class," Kori added quickly when Zach opened his mouth in what she could only assume was protest. He closed it again and nodded.

At the sound and sight of people, Ibis jumped off the couch and ran to greet them and receive some petting. Kori dug out a couple of bowls and filled one up with food and the other with water and placed them on the kitchen floor while Zach received kisses from Ibis.

"What a friendly dog," he said.

Kori gave him a quick history of her past—the little that she knew—and then they endured a brief silence that was only mildly awkward.

"I had a really good—" Kori started.

"Last night was—" Zach said at exactly the same time.

They both paused and laughed, Kori's shoulders relaxing a little.

"Go ahead," Zach said.

"I had a really good time last night. Thank you for that." She smiled shyly.

"Last night was perfect. I wouldn't have wanted to change anything."

Kori looked back up at Zach's face and saw that he was smiling from ear to ear. She was relieved that they were completely on the same page. Maybe Nora was right about Lani Silver being no threat to their relationship.

"Can I get you something to drink?" she asked.

He shook his head. "I'm actually here on unofficial business." He paused and Kori's heart leapt into her throat. The last time he came to her on unofficial business she'd been a suspect—the main suspect—in a murder case. "Remember when we were working through Tessa's murder?"

She nodded. This was sounding worse and worse.

"We had to take a sample of your DNA as evidence so it's now in the database. Scoter Circle's police department contacted us this afternoon to let us know that they had a family hit with your DNA. We'll be working with them on a murder case."

Kori could feel the blood drain from her face. "What do you mean you had a family hit?"

"It means that there was DNA at the crime scene that we know was a relative of yours. We know it's not yours," he quickly added. "But we're looking for someone who's your relative. A male relative."

CHAPTER 3

Kori sat in the nearest chair, mouth hanging open. She quickly realized that and closed it without saying anything. Finally she asked, "Who was the victim?"

"I can't tell you that."

"If I guessed could you tell me yes or no?"

"Off the record," he said slowly. She knew she was putting him in a tough spot.

"Was it Heidi Fischer?"

Zach didn't say anything or give any indication that she was wrong. She couldn't imagine that there were two murders in the last few days in Scoter Circle. It was as small as Hermit Cove.

"If it was Heidi Fischer, blink twice," she said. She needed it to be confirmed.

Zach blinked twice and looked her in the eye. "This doesn't look good if you know who it was."

"You know I wasn't there. I was with you last night and working all morning!"

"I need to ask you this then, off the record: what do you know about Heidi Fischer and how do you know she was killed yesterday morning?"

Kori knew she'd put herself in a tough spot now. If there was male DNA from someone in her family, the only person she could think of was Jay. But he couldn't—he wouldn't—have killed her, killed anyone.

"Kori, this is all off the record," Zach said, putting his hand on her knee.

"Jay told me. He knew she was killed yesterday morning."

"That's what I was afraid of."

Kori looked up in horror. "What do you mean you were afraid of that?" Had Jay already become a suspect? Was he the *main* suspect?

"He's the only male relative of yours I know. So what other conclusion could I come to?"

Kori nodded. She'd gone there herself. "What happened? How was she killed?"

"Gunshot wound to the head."

"Are you sure it wasn't suicide?" she asked hopefully.

"It was ruled out immediately. Gunshot was to the left temple but she was right handed which immediately meant that there was only a slight chance it would have been suicide. And there was no gunshot residue on her hands which completely ruled that out."

Kori nodded again. She'd known they would have ruled it out if it was clear but had needed to ask.

"Kori, where is Jay now?"

She shook her head, looking down. "I don't know. I saw him at lunch. He was freaking out about Heidi's murder. But I haven't heard from him since."

"Can you call him?" Zach asked, both hands on her knees now, standing directly in front of her.

Kori looked up, tears threatening to spill over her eyes. "Please don't make me do that."

Zach nodded. "I won't. But I can't promise anything once Scoter Circle police talk to you. Or him."

"I know. I just can't be the one to lead you to him. I know he's innocent. I can't put him through an interrogation like I went through. It was awful."

Zach nodded and Kori leaned forward, resting her head against his broad chest. She needed to get strength from somewhere and it wasn't going to be from herself right now.

Ibis must have sensed her need because she came into the kitchen and calmly sat next to her. Kori reached down and stroked her head, thankful that she'd finally caved today and adopted a dog.

"Would it have to be Jay? Could it be a cousin? An uncle?" Kori asked, suddenly sitting straight up again.

Zach shook his head. "It's possible. Let's make a list of all your male relatives. And it doesn't mean he's guilty, just that his DNA is there. We'll have to question him."

Kori got up from the stool she'd been sitting on and got herself a glass of water, a pad of paper and a pen. "I'll start with Jay. We both know him. And my dad's dead so unless there's something really weird going on, it's not him."

"What about cousins?" Zach asked, standing next to Kori as she wrote.

"My mom was an only child so I didn't have any cousins on her side. Dad had a sister. I don't even know the last time I thought about her, never mind saw her. They didn't have a close relationship and I guess that was passed on to us. But she had two kids, older than Jay and me. They were Tyler and Janie, a boy and a girl. I'll have to dig to find out where Tyler is now. This might sound crazy, but I hope it's him and not Jay."

"Obviously," Zach said, laughing. "No one wants their brother to be a murderer."

"No one wants their cousin to be a murderer either."

Zach nodded his agreement.

Kori paused, thinking about the best way to approach this situation with Jay. Finally she said, "Okay. I'll call him."

"Really? You will?" She could hear the surprise in Zach's voice. Apparently he'd stopped hoping.

"But I have to be there when he's questioned. I'll ask him to come here. For a beer."

Zach agreed and Kori made the call. They waited anxiously for the half hour it took for Jay to finish whatever he was doing and get to her house. When he finally arrived, Kori breathed a sigh of relief that he hadn't stood her up and made himself look guilty.

"Hey Jay. Thanks for coming over. Beer?" Kori asked, holding a bottle out to him without waiting for a response.

"Thanks. What's up?" he asked, suspicion on his face.

"I told Zach the only way I'd call you was if I was here when he talked to you—"

"Is this about Heidi?" he asked accusingly.

Kori nodded and Zach came into the kitchen.

"I thought you knew I was innocent?" He sounded betrayed.

"I *do* know you're innocent—" Kori protested but was interrupted.

"Jay, I wanted to talk to you before anything goes on the record," Zach started. "I told Kori that our office was contacted by the Scoter Circle police because there was a hit on a DNA match for Heidi Fischer's murder. A familial DNA match for someone in the system. That someone was Kori. We had her DNA because of Tessa's murder. And we know that the DNA they found was from a male relative. And, well—"

"So you're telling me that *my* DNA was at the scene of Heidi Fischer's murder?" Jay asked, his voice rising with each word.

"No. I'm saying that there was a familial match for a male related to Kori. And you're our first option. So you can willingly give me a sample now and I'll get it processed, or you can wait until Scoter Circle arrests you."

"Wow. Really leaving me a lot of options. What do you need for a DNA sample? And what about our cousin, Tyler?" Jay asked, turning to look at Kori.

"We just talked about that. Do you know where he is, what he's been doing? Kori said she hasn't kept in touch with him."

Jay shook his head. "I haven't either. He was older. We never really got to know his family."

Zach nodded and took a long Q-tip from his pocket. "Open up. This will only take a second and I'll get it processed right away." Zach glanced at the clock. "I have a half hour to get it back to the station."

Jay did as he was told and Zach had his sample in thirty seconds.

"Okay. I'll give you a call when I know," he said and headed for the door.

Kori followed him downstairs and out of ear shot of Jay. "Zach, you don't really think it's Jay, do you? What else do you have on him?"

"No, I don't really think it's him. But this doesn't look good. I'll be honest with you about that. But the fact that he willingly gave his DNA is a good sign. We'll either confirm that he was there or that he wasn't. The only other thing we have is his online relationship with Heidi from a couple years ago. We don't have a motive. We'll know which direction to go when we get these results."

"And then you'll find Tyler?"

"I'll start looking. You'll do the same?" Zach asked.

Kori nodded. "Will you get the results tonight?"

"I'll put a rush on them, but I make no promises."

"And if it's not his DNA—?"

Zach shrugged. "Then we move on to Tyler and whatever other leads come up."

Kori gave Zach a quick kiss on the cheek and he turned to leave. Kori walked back upstairs and found Jay with his head in his hands on the same stool she'd sat on less than an hour earlier.

"Tell me more about your relationship with Heidi—everything you know about her," Kori requested and flipped to the next page on the pad of paper she'd been using. She picked up her pen and was ready to take notes. If she was going to solve this mystery and clear her brother's name like she'd cleared her own she was going to need to know every last detail.

Jay looked up. "Get me another beer. Then I'll tell you everything I know about her."

Kori grabbed two more from the fridge, popped the tops off of them and sat on the stool next to Jay.

"Heidi Fischer. What caught me first was her looks. You know I'm a sucker for red hair. She had long red hair. I couldn't *not* check out her profile. And what I read was too good not to contact her."

"What caught your attention?" Kori asked before he could overlook those details.

"She had two dogs. She'd grown up in Scoter Circle. She loved music—*loved* it. So I messaged her through the dating site. I learned that she was divorced. No kids. She played the piano. That was her true passion. But she was also a teller at a bank. She was trying to move up in the bank so she could make enough money to save and then be able to retire early so she could focus on her music."

"How long did you guys message back and forth?"

"Only about a week. Then we started calling each other. I hate talking on the phone but it was easy with her. We'd talk everyday almost. And for at least an hour."

"What'd you talk about?"

Jay got a faraway look in his eyes like he was remembering good times. "Everything. And nothing. Her work. Mine. Our families.

Where she'd traveled. How I never did. Music. Books. Hermit Cove. Scoter Circle. Nothing that really sticks out. But there wasn't anything we couldn't talk about. You know?"

Kori did. She felt that way with Zach. Their conversations were always easy and any silences weren't awkward. "It sounds like you have only good memories of her. What made you stop talking to her?"

"She got back together with her ex. She was pregnant I learned after a few months and they were going to give it another shot. She'd gotten pregnant after they divorced but he was the father."

"Do you know anything about him? Could he have wanted her dead?"

"I don't know. I only know his name—Brett Carr."

Kori snapped into action, grabbing her laptop from the coffee table and bringing it back to the kitchen.

"What are you doing?" Jay asked.

"Looking up Brett Carr. We need to know everything about him. Did he own a gun that he used to kill Heidi? Does he have past criminal charges? Was he still with Heidi? If he had a motive, he would be on the suspect list."

"Wouldn't the police already have questioned him?"

"Who knows? I think Zach is great. But I don't know that the police can really do their work well with all the bureaucracy that goes on behind the scenes."

Even with Jay barely interested in clearing his own name, Kori pulled up Google and typed in *Brett Carr*. She got hits from all over the country so narrowed it down to *Brett Carr Scoter Circle*.

She was rewarded with plenty of information and she started opening web pages to sift through it all. Jay finally came out of his depressed daze and stood behind her reading over her shoulder.

"Here's an article from six months ago about him getting into a fight at a bar." Kori kept skimming. "It doesn't say what it was about or who started it, but he could be associated with shady people."

"Or he could have been in the wrong place at the wrong time. We don't know what really happened," Jay protested.

Kori turned around and looked at her brother. "Do you want to find out who really killed Heidi or do you want to spend the rest of your life in prison for a crime you didn't commit?"

"You're right," he said with more passion. "Let's see what else he has a history of."

Kori returned to the newspaper articles she had opened and moved on to the next one.

"Nine months ago he was arrested but not convicted of a hit and run. Maybe he knows someone in law enforcement to have gotten that charge dropped." Kori moved on to the next article. "And here, just over a year ago, he was accused of attempted robbery but was again released without a conviction. This guy looks like bad news."

"What about a gun? Does he own one?" Jay asked.

"I don't know how to look that up. We'll let Zach know to look into that. Do *you* even have a gun?"

Zach looked down at the floor and nodded.

"Since when?" Kori asked, shocked.

"Dad took me to the shooting range a few times when we were kids. When he died he left me his. I've never even used it."

"Do you know where it is? Could someone have used your gun to kill Heidi?"

The look of fear Jay had worn earlier returned. "I don't know. I haven't really kept tabs on it."

"I think you need to go home and check on it."

CHAPTER 4

Kori spent a significant part of her evening looking up whatever information she could find about both Brett Carr and Heidi Fischer. She figured finding Tyler would be easier so she focused on the harder tasks for the moment.

As she suspected from their different last names, Heidi and Brett were not married. They'd remained divorced after Jay's relationship with Heidi. They did have a kid together, but Kori couldn't find any information about that.

Beyond what Jay had shared about Heidi, Kori was also unable to find any other potentially useful information. She eventually called it a night. Ibis looked at her new dog bed, then gave Kori sad eyes. Kori laughed, patted the bed next to her and let Ibis curl up next to her on the bed instead of on the new dog bed on the floor.

Ibis seemed to know that Kori was an early riser, because just minutes before her alarm was set to go off, Ibis crawled closer and started licking Kori's face.

"Good morning to you too. You have to go out?"

At the mention of going out, Ibis leaped off the bed and raced toward the stairs down to the café.

"Okay. But you have to give me a few minutes first."

Kori put on yesterday's jeans and a clean t-shirt and headed to the bathroom. She was faster than usual, not wanting Ibis to have to wait too long, and then grabbed the leash Vera had given her and took Ibis outside.

They walked up and down Main Street in the early morning quiet. It was refreshingly chilly and Kori was soon wide awake and ready for her day.

Back inside, she quickly went back upstairs and brought down one of the dog beds. She put it in her office at the back of the kitchen where she would easily be able to keep an eye on Ibis throughout the day. She hoped that she wouldn't have to take Ibis out until she closed.

Ibis happily lay on the bed and watched Kori work. The dough she'd prepped Sunday afternoon was risen and ready for baking. She turned the oven on high and got out her Dutch ovens.

While the oven preheated, she assembled the breakfast casseroles—potatoes, eggs, and veggies for the vegetarian casserole and potatoes, eggs, fewer veggies and plenty of bacon for the meat lovers.

She stuck the bread in the oven and then got the pancake batter ready, slicing bananas that she would add to each individual pancake as they cooked.

Just as the bread was coming out of the oven and she turned down the temperature for the breakfast casseroles, the front door opened and she looked up. It was exactly who she expected—her mother, Gale.

"Morning, Mom," she called before the front door had even closed.

Gale hurried into the kitchen, helped herself to orange juice from the fridge and then launched into what Kori knew was coming—a crisis. "You will *never* guess what happened this weekend."

Instead of indulging her mother, Kori told her, "Jay told me you went to Scoter Circle for the weekend."

Gale nodded, eyes wide, as she chugged the juice. "And you'll *never* guess what happened when I was there."

Kori knew her mother didn't actually want her to guess. "What happened?" she asked instead of telling her what she already knew was coming.

"There was a murder." Gale waited for Kori to react.

"No." Kori put on her best shocked voice for her mother's benefit.

"I knew you wouldn't believe me. But check the papers. Someone name Heidi Fischer."

Kori decided to continue her front of ignorance and find out any details her mother would divulge. She knew she'd be more likely to talk if she thought Kori didn't know anything.

"Who's Heidi Fischer?"

"So it turns out she worked at a bank, some high up position." Kori noted that she must have quickly worked her way up the ranks if just two years ago she'd been a teller. "But she had a long history of online relationships. So they're looking into all of those men, thinking that one of them might have been using her to launder money or get access to the security vault or a safety deposit box. The talk was that she knew something illegal was going on at the bank but was being manipulated by one of her online boyfriends. Can you believe that? The way dating has gone for your generation."

"Mm hmm," Kori mumbled, wishing she could write down everything her mother had just told her. "Were there any specific suspects or just anyone who knew her?"

"I don't know. The only thing I heard about was her online dating past."

Kori suspected that wasn't the only thing she heard but the only thing she chose to focus on.

"You don't know any of her past online boyfriends?" Kori asked.

Gale shook her head. "I never met the woman. Just heard people talking."

"Why'd you go to Scoter Circle anyway?"

"Yoga retreat. And you'll never guess who was leading it!" The excitement in her mother's voice was palpable.

"No? Who?" Kori asked. This time she had no idea of the answer.

"Heidi's ex-husband, Brett Carr. I personally think he did it and used the yoga retreat as a cover up. No one would look to a yogi as a murderer. And he was supposedly at the retreat all weekend. But it would have been plenty easy to slip out for an hour. I even did!"

Kori was intensely interested. Not only did Brett have a history of violence, but he seemed to have an alibi. But not an air tight alibi perhaps. And what about a motive?

"How was Brett? Why do you think he did it?"

"Well, after Heidi was killed, I heard people talking about the child support he had to pay. Since he was well off and had a great job— yoga is a side business, I don't know what he does but everyone said he's a millionaire—he had to make huge payments every month."

"If he was making such large child support payments, why was Heidi still working?" Something didn't line up with what Jay had told her about Heidi wanting to work her way up at the bank and retire early. Had she just played Brett into having a kid with her so she'd make easy money? But then why was she still working? Maybe Gale's story about Heidi being involved in shady business at the bank was true.

"That was a big question everyone was asking." Gale looked at the clock. "I've gotta run! Anita doesn't wait for anyone at spin. She gets started whether the class is full or not."

Gale walked quickly to the front door and waved goodbye. Kori hadn't even had a chance to introduce her to the new family member, Ibis, who was sleeping quietly in the office. She was turning out to be the perfect café dog if she didn't even bark or get up when someone she didn't know came in.

Kori checked the casseroles and then turned the sign on the door to open, leaving the door unlocked. Then she started slicing the still-warm bread and got out all of the jams that she and Nora had made last summer. She was getting down to the last jars and was looking forward to refilling them soon. It was only a month until Nora's strawberries would be producing and she'd spend her afternoons harvesting them for her.

Just after six, Jay walked through the door. Kori was glad that it was a quiet morning so far so she could sit and talk to Jay about anything he'd found out—and the status of his gun—and what their mother had shared with her. But the look on his face was anything but calm and she knew he had bad news for her.

"I don't know where my gun is," he said, panicking.

"What do you mean? When was the last time you saw it?" she asked, pouring two mugs of coffee and placing them across from each other in a booth. Jay sat and picked one up, taking a long swallow.

"I haven't shot it in years, since Dad was alive. I never even thought about it until you brought it up last night. I don't know the last time I saw it." Jay hung his head, clearly stressed about his possibly missing gun.

"Where did you used to keep it?"

"I thought it was hidden in my closet. But it isn't there. So I checked my home office, my car, the kitchen—"

Kori chuckled, trying to lighten the mood. "Why would it be in your kitchen?"

Jay shrugged. "I don't know. I just tore my house apart looking for it."

"Can you think of anyone who might have had access to it?"

"No. I never talked about it. Clearly I didn't even know where I kept it so I wouldn't have told anyone where it was. I have no idea. What if it was the gun that killed Heidi?"

Just then the front door opened and Kori got up to greet her new customers—Zach and Lani.

"Morning. What can I get for you?" she asked, her heart leaping at the sight of Zach. She made sure to remind herself about the last two nights and Nora's reassuring words that there was no way Lani would be able to get him to notice her looks.

"Just coffee, thanks. Jay, can we join you?" Zach asked, not waiting for a response and sliding into the booth opposite him. Lani followed suit.

"Did you get the results of the DNA?" Jay asked hopefully.

"Yeah. And it's relatively good news. It's not a perfect match. So Scoter Circle Police Department is looking for a second sample since they couldn't rule you out as a suspect or confirm that you were there. They think it could have been contaminated."

Jay sighed.

Just then, the morning rush finally started. Teddi West was the first in the crowd and ordered just a coffee to go. He opened the Hermit Market pretty early and probably had to get to work right away.

Spencer Graff and Derek Spears came in with Betsy Scoop and they all sat together in a booth. Following them were two families visiting Hermit Cove and Kori was cooking breakfasts as quickly as she could to keep up.

As expected, the bacon-filled breakfast casserole was a hit. Many customers ordered a side of toast, so her bread was quickly running low as well. Midway through the morning she had to make a second bacon casserole and put it in the oven before the first ran out.

Ibis was quiet all morning. Every time Kori looked her way, Ibis was intently watching Kori work. But she never barked and not once showed interest in being with the customers. Kori was confident that if Ibis was in the dining area she would have acted the same way but she'd give her a longer trial time to make sure.

Just before Kori was about to close, Jay walked back inside. "Hey. You look more relaxed than I've seen you in a couple days," Kori said, wiping the last of the tables. "Turn that sign around for me, would you?"

Jay did as asked and sat back in the same booth they'd shared that morning. Kori made her way to him and sat across.

"What's up?" she asked.

"I was able to hack into Heidi's online dating profile to get a better idea of the guys she was connected to."

Kori hadn't had a chance that morning to update Jay on their mother's findings so she did so now, sharing every detail she could remember. When she was finished, Jay said, "Well, I found the three most recent guys she talked to or dated. There's Wesley Sanders who works on Wall Street but is from Scoter Circle, Oscar Baer who is Brett's cousin—who dates their ex-husband's cousin or their cousin's ex-wife?—and Larry Downing who is a billionaire in Scoter Circle but I couldn't find out anything about how he came into that money."

"Do you know any of them?" Kori asked. "Anyone who could have gotten their hands on your gun? Or your DNA?"

"We don't even know that my gun was the weapon that was used or that it's even my DNA. But no, I don't know any of them. Maybe it's time to track down Tyler."

Just then, Gale walked in with a whirlwind of energy.

"Oh good. Jay, you're here. I just stopped by the Auto Body looking for you and Spencer didn't know where you'd gone. I know my kids so well." She walked over to their booth and kissed Jay on the cheek. "How was business today?" she asked, turning to Kori.

"Good. How was spin class?"

"Oh, you wouldn't believe it. We had four intervals with only short rests. I didn't think I was going to finish it!"

Kori didn't know how she and Jay had turned out so calm when their mother was such a drama queen.

"But anyway, Jay, I was looking for you because I'd borrowed your gun a couple weeks ago to take to a shooting range and I wanted to return it."

Jay's mouth dropped open. "Mom, when did you take it?" he asked, giving Kori a knowing glance.

"Oh I don't know, two, three weeks ago? It had just been in the coffee table drawer. I didn't think you'd miss it. I've had it in my car so I could give it back to you whenever I saw you. But I never did!"

"No, I didn't miss it—"

Kori could tell that Jay was going to keep talking and tell Gale about Heidi's gunshot wound to the head but she cut him off before he could. "Don't you think you should have let him know you'd taken it?" Kori asked.

"Oh, you two. You're always so clingy with your stuff. I'm your mother. We shared everything when you were growing up. That shouldn't have to change just because you don't live with me anymore."

Kori rolled her eyes and crossed her fingers that Jay wouldn't pursue the topic.

"Well, here you go." Gale nonchalantly handed Jay the gun. "I used it last week at the shooting range so it's empty."

"Thanks," Jay said, sounding stunned.

"Mom, before you go, have you kept in touch with Dad's sister or Tyler and Janie at all?" Kori asked, making Gale turn back toward them and stop walking to the door.

"Not really. Why do you ask?" The expression on her face didn't convey complete trust.

"Oh, you know . . ." Kori stalled for time, trying to come up with an excuse. "We're not getting any younger and they're the only extended family we have. I just thought it'd be nice to get to know them maybe."

"Well isn't that nice. But no, I haven't been in touch with any of them for years. I'm not sure where they're even living now. Ever since your father had that falling out with his sister all those years ago, I hardly heard anything when he was still alive. And once he was gone—I don't think they even came to his funeral. Trust me, you're better off without them."

Gale waved her hand and turned back to the door.

As soon as she was gone Jay turned to Kori, completely ignoring the comments about their extended family, and said, "This means that my gun was in Scoter Circle this weekend. And with my DNA possibly at the crime scene, this has gone from bad to worse."

CHAPTER 5

"What time is it?" Kori asked Jay, letting her mind race away from her while trying to devise a plan.

Jay glanced at his watch. "Almost one thirty. Why?"

"I think we need to go for a drive. Come on." Kori heard Ibis walk toward their table from the kitchen where she had been sleeping. She looked like she was asking if she was invited. "Ibis, let's go."

"Where are we going?" Jay got up and followed Kori who was on a mission and Ibis who was at her heels. She noticed that he grabbed his gun from the table where their mother had placed it. She hoped that he would find a secure place for it when he got home and start keeping tabs on it. Guns weren't something he should be so careless about.

"We're going to Scoter Circle."

"What? What are we going to do there?"

Kori held the door open for Jay and Ibis, locked it behind her and then led the way to her car. "We're going to start asking the questions that need to be answered."

"Don't you have work to do?" Jay jogged to catch up. Kori was walking too fast.

"Yes. But it can wait. Family comes first. And it looks like you need to get some more information before you get arrested."

"Shouldn't you just call Zach and tell him to do this?"

Kori couldn't figure out why Jay needed so much convincing to solve this murder that he was constantly looking more and more guilty of committing.

"I could. But then he'd have to go through too many hoops to get where he needs to be. Where we need to be. Get in." Kori had unlocked her car and was holding the driver's door open, ready to get in and drive away but Jay was still hesitating. Ibis jumped into the open door and headed to the back seat where she happily lay down. "Are you worried about missing work?" she asked.

Jay nodded slightly.

"Don't be. Spencer will understand. Call him on the way. Let's go."

Jay finally opened the door and sat in the passenger seat, still looking stunned. "Who are we even going to talk to?"

Kori didn't really have a plan. "Well, there are the three guys you found who we could look into. You said Larry Downing lives in Scoter Circle?" Jay nodded and Kori started the car, glanced at him for his answer and backed out of her parking spot behind the café. She was always thankful she didn't have to deal with parallel parking on Main Street. There wasn't much traffic, but there weren't many parking spots either. "We could start with him. And Brett Carr. He might be easier to approach. We can tell him Mom was at his yoga retreat and she's having some muscle pain now. Ask him about the weekend. See if there were any gaps in classes or when he could have been gone."

"Okay."

"And while I drive, try to find Tyler. He's our cousin, we should be able to figure out how to contact him."

Jay obediently took out his phone and waited for more instructions. "Where should I start?"

"I don't know. Facebook. Are you friends with him? Or Janie?"

"I don't think so. Hang on."

Kori drove and waited for Jay's answer. How could it be so difficult to locate their cousin? Unless, of course, he didn't want to be found because he had something to hide.

After some silence, Jay finally said, "Here we go, Tyler Roberts. Wow, he looks nothing like the last time we saw him."

"Well it has to be at least fifteen years. No, less. Dad's funeral? No, Mom said they didn't come. Wow, maybe it has been that long. You're sure it's him? What can you see about him?" Kori was desperate for information.

"Almost nothing."

"Friend him," Kori instructed and she saw Jay fiddle with his phone out of the corner of her eye. "Let's hope he uses Facebook often enough to see it and accept it right away."

They drove on in silence. Kori was planning her next move to clear Jay's name, and her next move with Zach. She wanted to go out with him again but she didn't want to seem too eager either. Oh, who was she kidding? They'd been playing this game since high school. And being eager was probably important with Lani working next to him all day. She'd call him tonight and invite him hiking next weekend. Or, better yet, she'd invite him to Nora's farm stand opening on Wednesday. It was always a potluck dinner that kicked off the town's gardening season. Really, just Nora's public gardening season. Kori bought plenty of vegetables from her but there were always extra. Kori had done every year since she'd moved back to Hermit Cove and had even come up a couple times for it when she was living in New York City. All of their friends from childhood went and the food was always better than expected. Kori would even offer to do the cooking for both of them so Zach wouldn't have to bring anything. He wouldn't have an excuse then.

"He accepted," Jay suddenly said, breaking through Kori's daydreaming of officially dating Zach and becoming his girlfriend.

"Oh good," Kori said excitedly. "Check out his photos. Where does he live? Has he been to Scoter Circle recently? Does he know Heidi?" The questions poured out of her mouth before Jay had a chance to answer even the first one.

"Umm . . . give me a few seconds . . . Here it is. According to Facebook he lives on the west coast. About as far from Scoter Circle as he could get and still be in the United States. What else did you want to know?"

"Mutual friends. Do you two have any mutual friends?"

She saw Jay flipping through Facebook as she continued driving. "No. Not even you."

"If I'd already been friends with him do you think it would have been so hard to find him?"

"Right. But anyway," Jay said sarcastically, "he's not friends with Heidi. What if he didn't even know her? What if it's not his DNA there and it really is mine? Who would set me up?"

"That's what we're here to find out," Kori said with false confidence.

"Here where? Where are you going?" Jay asked as she sped past the turn she wanted into Scoter Circle.

"Oops." She pulled over and turned around.

"Where are we going to go when we get there?"

"Let's start with the yoga retreat location. Mom said it was at the conference center. Have you ever been there?"

"No." Jay pulled out his phone to get directions.

On Kori's second try she didn't miss the turn and they were only minutes from Scoter Circle's center. "Where to now?"

"Umm. Turn right onto Willow Lane. It looks like the conference center is down there."

Kori did as instructed and they found their location with no trouble. Kori parked in the buzzing parking lot and got out of the car, knowing she'd figure out what she was going to say once she reached the front desk. Jay hesitated but eventually got out too.

"Just follow my lead," she told him with more false confidence. Turning back to Ibis, she said, "Don't bark. We'll be quick." Then she felt ridiculous.

Kori opened the front door to the conference center and was immediately struck by a swarm of police walking up and down the main hallway. She stopped in her tracks and she felt Jay bump into her.

"What's going on, you think?" she asked him.

He shook his head and didn't say anything so she led the way up to the front desk.

"Good afternoon. How may I help you?" a short woman wearing a nametag that identified her as Meri asked, a cheerful smile on her face.

"Um. Hi. What's going on?" Kori asked, still looking around.

"All I know is that this has been turned into a crime scene and police are working on getting everything worked through as quickly as possible. Are you here for the travel symposium? There's only a short delay for it to begin."

"No. No. We're actually looking for Brett Carr. He led a yoga retreat here this weekend and we were hoping he was still around."

"I'm sorry. He was here this weekend but doesn't work here regularly." Meri's smile turned into a look of concern for being unable to help Kori and Jay.

"Would it be possible to get us in touch with him? Does he live in town? Our mother attended his retreat and is now having some difficulty with her shoulder. We were just hoping to ask him a few questions about how she could fix that."

"You know, normally I can't do that. But let me call him and see if he's available to come in."

"That'd be really great. Thanks." Kori was relieved. With the added chaos of a police investigation she thought they might have made the drive for nothing.

"Just take a seat," Meri indicated chairs across the hall from the desk, "and I'll let you know when I reach him."

Meri picked up the phone while Jay and Kori walked to the offered chairs and took in the scene.

Police were whispering in the halls, some running back and forth from one end to the other. Kori was surprised they were even allowed inside.

"I'm going to go check on Ibis. Text me if Meri tells you anything," Kori told Jay who nodded his acceptance and she walked outside to her car.

Ibis was still calmly sleeping in the back seat, seemingly unaware of the panic that Kori felt growing inside of her. Why would Jay have been setup? And what had Gale done this weekend? Was she somehow involved? What was this current crime scene in the conference center? Kori suspected it was unrelated to Heidi's murder but she couldn't be too sure about anything anymore.

When Kori opened the back door to let Ibis out, she quickly hooked the leash on her and started walking toward the road. She planned to just bring her around the block on the sidewalk to get her moving. She checked her pocket for a plastic bag in case she had any business to take care of but she came up empty. She'd have to make that become part of her normal routine now—always have something to clean up after Ibis.

Kori and Ibis barely made it a hundred yards from the conference center's parking lot when Kori's phone buzzed in her pocket. She figured it was Jay telling her to come back inside because Brett was on his way.

"Hello?" she answered without bothering to look at the name on the screen.

"Kori? It's Zach. Where are you? I'm outside The Early Bird and you're not there."

She didn't want to tell him the truth because he wouldn't like what she was up to but she couldn't imagine lying to him. She decided on being vague. "I had to help Jay with something. What's up?"

"I was just stopping by for a cup of coffee with the most beautiful chef in town."

Kori's heart fluttered and she wondered if she was having a heart attack. She couldn't help but smile. "I can stop by your place later if you want." So much for waiting to see him at Nora's opening.

"I'm not sure when I'll be home. This case that Scoter Circle has us working on is getting the best of my time. I really only had a few minutes and hoped I'd be able to fill them with your face."

Kori blushed. "Have you gotten any more information about the DNA?"

"Nope. Sorry. I'll keep you posted."

"Great. Thanks. Hey, do you have plans on Wednesday night? Nora's farm stand is opening for the season and I was hoping you'd come with me. She has a potluck dinner every year to kick off the season. I can cook for both of us if—"

"Sounds great," Zach said, cutting her off before she could make any excuses for him. She could hear the smile in his voice at the other end of the line.

"Great. I'll see you Wednesday then."

"Wednesday."

Kori waited to see if he was going to say anything else but heard the phone click off instead. She smiled.

But she didn't have time to revel in her next date because her phone started buzzing again. This time she looked at the caller— Jay.

She picked up and he was already talking. "Come back. He's on his way. He'll be here any minute."

"Okay. On my way." Kori hung up and turned to bring Ibis back to the car. As they walked into the parking lot a car tore past them and parked in a hurry. She wondered if that was Brett, so instead of making him wait she decided to bring Ibis with her.

As soon as Kori opened the front door, Jay got up to meet her and Meri rushed out from behind the desk. In an overly friendly voice Meri said, "I'm sorry, ma'am, but you can't bring your dog in here."

"Oh, sorry. She's actually a retired therapy dog so she won't bother anyone," Kori protested. She really didn't want to miss talking to Brett.

"Even so, it's our policy that dogs aren't allowed inside unless they're assistance animals."

Kori turned and looked behind her. The driver of the in-a-hurry car was now speed walking toward the front door. It was a man and she could only assume it was Brett.

"I promise she won't bother anyone," Kori insisted again, not having a clue if that was true or not. She'd barely had her for a full day. "I'll just stay in the lobby."

Meri looked past Kori at the man approaching. "Mr. Carr, thank you for coming in. This is Kori—I'm not sure I got your last name?"

"Cooke. Kori Cooke."

"This is Kori Cooke and Jay," Meri paused, letting Jay share his last name.

"Cooke," he said.

"Kori, Jay. Call me Brett," Brett said, not quite unfriendly but also not very inviting. He walked past them inside and Kori followed him before Meri could stop her.

Brett turned left when he reached the front desk and then let himself into a small meeting room. The police had mostly congregated at the other end of the hall and had finally taped off everything to the right of the front desk.

Brett, Kori and Jay all took seats around a small table and Ibis lay quietly at Kori's feet. She was glad Meri didn't come looking for them, and that Ibis didn't make a sound to bring attention to her presence.

"I understand you had some questions about the yoga retreat I led this weekend," Brett said, getting straight to the point. Kori was thankful for that. There really was no point in small talk.

"Yes. Our mother was a participant and she's having some back and neck pain now. We wondered if there was anything in particular that could have caused that and what she can do now to get rid of it," Kori said, feeling funny that she was lying so confidently.

"Did she come with you so I could talk to her about it directly?" he asked, unsmiling.

Kori and Jay both shook their heads.

"Well, there's really little information that I can give you then. I'd recommend seeing a chiropractor if it doesn't get better in a few days. But I was only there in the afternoons. So any of the morning sessions I wasn't a part of and am unfamiliar with."

Kori was surprised her mother hadn't told her that detail. Gale had said Brett was there all day every day, hadn't she? The timing of Heidi's murder lined up with Brett's absences from classes. What was Gale hiding by pinning the murder on him but omitting that scheduling detail?

"Well, thank you for your time then." Kori wasn't quite sure how to ask him about Heidi's death without giving away too much information. She figured this one piece of information was worth it and let any other interrogation go. She stood and offered her hand, which he shook. Jay did the same.

"Sorry to be so unhelpful. I hope that your mother is feeling better soon."

With that, Brett made a speedy exit and Kori tailed him back to the parking lot. She noticed Meri give her a dirty look as she led Ibis back outside but she ignored her.

"That wasn't really that helpful," Jay said, walking quickly to keep up again.

"Shh. Just get in the car," Kori whispered back, never taking her eye off Brett.

As soon as he started his car, Kori did the same and then followed him out of the parking lot. He turned away from the main road— the opposite way than they'd come in—and Kori did the same.

"Where are we going now?" Jay asked.

"I'm going to follow him. Find out where he lives so I can come back if I need to and find him at home."

"This is ridiculous. You're going to get yourself in trouble. Don't we have enough trouble right now for the Cooke family?"

Kori ignored her brother's concerns and stayed a block behind Brett's car. She was thankful that she drove a nondescript silver Subaru sedan that he'd be unlikely to notice.

It was only minutes before he pulled into a short driveway, parked and got out of the car. A woman, well endowed in the looks department with measurements as close to Barbie as one could get and still be able to walk, came outside to greet him. Kori kept her eyes focused on the public display of affection as she drove past and then turned to look at Jay.

"Who do you think that was?" he asked.

"If I had to guess, Brett's motive for killing Heidi."

CHAPTER 6

"What do you mean?" Jay asked.

"You really don't watch detective shows, do you?" she teased. He shook his head. "If he never got back with Heidi, or they never remarried anyway, then he had to pay plenty of child support. Maybe Heidi wanted him back. Or was blackmailing him. Or was somehow preventing him from being with that blond bimbo. Or who knows what. Then he might have needed her out of the picture."

"Wouldn't he still have to pay child support in the form of raising his own kid?"

"You have a point. But maybe Heidi was getting it super inflated. Who knows? But I think it's suspicious that his ex-wife is dead—and who knows when they finally ended things—and he's already making out with someone else in his front yard."

"I guess you're right. How are we going to find out more about that?" Jay asked.

"Pull out your phone. See if you can find Heidi's obituary. It'll say who she outlived. And it might even tell us about a memorial service and funeral."

Kori continued driving, heading back home. It was already late afternoon and she had work to do and wanted to stop by Nora's so Ibis could meet Milo and Otis. She knew Ibis would need some dog friends for play dates after spending her mornings cooped up in the café. She waited for Jay to find what they were looking for.

"Here it is," he finally said. "Outlived by her son—doesn't give the name—and her parents. No mention of a husband."

"What about a service?" Kori asked.

"Tomorrow night, Tuesday. Just a memorial. No funeral until the investigation is closed."

"Perfect. Make sure you take tomorrow afternoon off. I think we have another trip to Scoter Circle we'll have to make."

"We're *going* to the memorial?" Jay asked. Kori could feel him shooting daggers at her from his eyes.

"Of course we're going. We'll see if we can get more information about her and her relationships from her friends. Find out more about her history with Brett. If he had a history of violence, maybe she was the target in the past."

"You really are crazy. What about Wesley, Oscar, Larry and Tyler? Can't we just focus on them instead?"

"We'll look into them, but Tyler doesn't have any connection to Heidi. And we're starting from zero with Wesley, Larry and Oscar. I think talking to her family and friends—and coworkers—will be our best shot at information."

Jay was silent for a moment while he digested Kori's plan. "Fine."

"Great. Look up Wesley while I drive home. I bet there's information about him on a company website or something. You said he works on Wall Street. He's not going to be anonymous online. I could call looking for investment advice. Or we could go to Heidi's bank and you could ask about her friends. You'd just have to play up being her boyfriend. We could even do that before the memorial tomorrow."

Kori snuck a glance at Jay and saw that he didn't particularly like the idea of that plan.

"Let's just get home for now. I have to go talk to Spencer about missing work this afternoon."

"Yeah sure. Think about it, though. I'll do some more research tonight."

Kori drove the rest of the way home brainstorming how she was going to get close to Oscar, Larry and Wesley to learn more. Just in case Brett didn't turn up guilty.

Back in Hermit Cove close to five o'clock, she dropped Jay off at the Auto Body and then went home. She headed straight to the café's kitchen to get things ready for tomorrow. Thankfully she still had plenty of eggs and greens from her visit to Nora the day before.

The smoothies continued to be a hit so she would offer them for a third day in a row. She decided to make overnight oatmeal with apples, cinnamon and a splash of syrup or brown sugar when it was served, so she got that all setup in the crock pot and turned it on.

For eggs, she'd make popovers again in the morning and offer veggie omelets. She had plenty of spinach, onions and mushrooms and she could even offer avocado on the first few lucky customers until they were gone. She didn't have many.

For her sweet-tooth customers, she assembled baked French toast that she'd stick in the oven tomorrow morning and she'd whip up pancake batter and slice bananas for either plain or banana pancakes again.

Satisfied with her menu, she brought Ibis outside and got back in the car to go to Nora's. As soon as she pulled up, Milo and Otis came storming out of the nearest greenhouse, likely smelling a new dog. Kori knew they would get along with any dog, but this was her first time introducing Ibis to a dog. Given her past, she was hopeful they would all get along.

Ibis immediately stood on the back seat, tail wagging, excitement in her eyes. Kori got out and greeted Milo and Otis, letting them smell her hands that were covered in Ibis' scent.

With all of the commotion, Nora came out of the same greenhouse the dogs had exited. "You got the dog?" she called with excitement.

"Yeah. I brought her over to meet Milo and Otis. And you of course!" Kori opened the back door and Ibis jumped out.

Nora walked over to Kori where the three dogs were sniffing each other before beginning a dog game of tag.

"Looks like they're already best friends," Kori said when Nora had reached her. The dogs were tearing circles around the yard.

"She'll sleep well tonight."

"Good. I need a good night's sleep too. I'm helping Jay find a murderer so he's not on a suspect list."

Nora turned to Kori and gave her a serious look. "I thought that was a onetime event when you investigated Tessa's murder."

"Yeah, so did I. But I can't just let Jay suffer through an investigation alone. He doesn't even seem interested in clearing his name."

Kori got Nora caught up on the last couple days' events, including Gale having Jay's gun in Scoter Circle at the time of Heidi's murder,

Jay's possible DNA found at the crime scene and their conversation with Brett that afternoon.

"Actually, speaking of Jay's gun, I don't think he took it out of the car when I dropped him off," Kori said, walking back toward her car to check the glove box where he'd left it. She opened it and saw that it was empty. "Well, it's not here so he must have." She changed the subject, needing something else to think about for a while. "Are you ready for the potluck on Wednesday?"

"Getting there. The farm stand is setup—did you see it at the bottom of the driveway?"

"I did. It looks great. Did you re-stain it this year?"

Nora nodded. "It was looking pretty worn out. And the RSVPs are coming in. It should be a good turnout. You're coming right?"

Kori blushed at the thought of Zach accompanying her and nodded.

"You're bringing Zach, aren't you?" Nora teased. "I can see it in your eyes. You're totally in love with him."

"Whoa whoa whoa. Don't go overboard! I think it'd be fun to call him my boyfriend, but let's not rush into *love*."

"Okay, whatever. I've gotta get back to work. I still have way too much to do before calling it a day."

Kori glanced at her watch and saw that it was already past six. "I should get Ibis home so we can both eat. We've each had a long day. See you Wednesday!" Kori turned back to the car and opened the back door for Ibis. Without even being called, she came running and flew into the back seat. "She must be hungry. Bye, Nora!"

"See ya. Good dog you got. I'm glad you finally caved."

"Me too." Kori waved, got in her car and drove home.

By the time she got home, she was already exhausted so didn't want to make anything fresh, but pulled out an already made bean burrito she'd wrapped in foil sometime in the past and frozen for just such an occasion.

Kori settled herself on the couch with her computer and burrito, ready to look into some more of the men Jay had put on his list of suspects. Ibis sat in front of her and looked up questioningly. Kori quickly invited her onto the couch and she knew she'd never be able to kick her off of it in the future. But she was fine with that. Ibis curled up at her feet and Kori got to work.

She pulled up Google and typed in *Wesley Sanders, Wall Street*. She was rewarded with plenty of hits and she began sifting through them.

She learned that Wesley had grown up in Scoter Circle with a single mom. There was no mention of his father. He went on to study at Yale University and fell in love with New York City on his weekends spent there.

He was ten years older than Kori and had lived in New York since he'd graduated from college. He'd been working in the New York Stock Exchange for sixteen years and had worked his way up the ladder. She easily found his photo and contact information listed on his company website. He looked completely harmless, but so did most criminals until she knew the truth about them.

She couldn't find anything that would have linked him to Heidi other than being from Scoter Circle. Did Wesley have an account at the same bank where Heidi worked? Was he a suspect who had already been cleared by now?

Kori decided to sleep on finding the answers to those questions. She had no idea how she was going to find out about a possible bank account but was confident that she'd have a better idea in the morning. Now, she was drained from her morning at work and afternoon of sleuthing with Jay.

"Come on, Ibis. You can sleep on the bed again." The second dog bed was maybe a waste of money for now, but she'd find a use for it she was sure.

Kori brushed her teeth, changed into pajamas and crawled between the sheets. Ibis curled up next to her and they were both asleep in minutes.

CHAPTER 7

At four in the morning, Kori's alarm sounded and she rubbed the sleep from her eyes. She'd slept hard and wasn't quite done yet. Her hand moved unconsciously to the other side of the bed and she found Ibis' warm body still curled next to her.

Ibis started at the feel of Kori's hand and jumped off the bed, instantly full of energy.

"I guess you're going to be my motivation this morning. You have to go out?" she asked her dog before she could stop herself from talking to her like she understood.

And maybe she did understand because she headed toward the door to the café. Kori found a clean pair of jeans and a fresh black t-shirt, quickly brushed her teeth and then followed Ibis downstairs. They walked to the front door and made a loop around the block, letting Ibis relieve herself before spending the morning in the office.

Once inside, Kori set to work. She got coffee brewing and could barely wait for it to be ready to pour herself a mug. She still felt tired.

Then she got started on the few things she had to get ready, starting with pancake batter. She made a double batch to start the morning, knowing she'd need more later on.

She checked the oatmeal she'd put in the crock pot last night and spooned herself a small bowl. She wasn't hungry yet but knew her stomach would start rumbling at exactly the wrong moment if she waited too long to eat something.

The baked French toast was all ready to be put in the oven so she turned on the heat and waited for it to reach the desired temperature, meanwhile making the popover batter.

Finally, she laid out all of the smoothie ingredients on the counter and got her blender out. She'd recently invested in plenty of Mason jars that fit onto her blender so she didn't have to keep pouring and washing the blender between orders. This way, she could blend straight into a Mason jar that became the serving container. She used this handy trick for crushing nuts, making vegetable purees and even to grind her own fresh cinnamon.

When she stuck the French toast in the oven, coffee was ready for drinking and she turned the closed sign to open and waited for her first customer.

In the quiet, Kori's mind wandered back to her research last night about Wesley Sanders. She needed to know if he had a bank account at Heidi's bank and if he'd been on the suspect list. Would the Scoter Circle Police Department keep that information from Zach if they were only worried about him finding information out about Jay?

Probably. She didn't have much faith in government departments working together. And that included different offices within the same department.

She glanced at the clock from the booth where she was sitting and saw that it was almost six, the time when she normally got busy. She stood up to refill her coffee mug and the door opened with her first customers.

"Zach. And Detective Silver. Good morning. What can I get you?" she asked, finding herself wishing that Zach had shown up alone.

"Hi Kori," Zach said with a smile. She couldn't help but match it. "I'll have a coffee and . . ." She saw him reading the menu. "Some oatmeal," he finally decided.

"I'll have coffee and banana pancakes," Detective Silver ordered.

"Let's talk while you cook," Zach said, heading to the counter in front of the window to the kitchen where Kori headed. She filled a bowl with oatmeal and gave them each an empty mug that they happily filled themselves.

"What's up?" Kori asked. She didn't know if Detective Silver knew about her past sleuthing and she was dying to ask Zach all the questions she wanted answered.

"We have something we wanted to talk to you about," Zach said, sitting down with his coffee.

"Is it about Jay? Because I'm not going to incriminate my own brother."

"It's about the case, but not necessarily about Jay."

"Well, since you brought up the case, I actually have something I wanted to talk to you about first, if that's okay," Kori said. She looked at Zach and Lani to gauge their reactions. "Do you know any of the other suspects?"

Zach remained silent. She knew he'd heard her but he was looking around to make sure no one else had come in yet.

"I do," he finally said.

"Is Brett Carr on the list?"

"How do you know about him?" he asked, Lani patiently observing the entire conversation.

"Jay knew he was Heidi's ex-husband," Kori explained.

"Right. Then, yes. He is."

"And Larry Downing?"

Kori was met with more silence.

"What do you know about him?" Zach finally asked.

"Nothing really. Just that he had been in touch with Heidi recently and lives in Scoter Circle."

"He's actually the reason we stopped by this morning."

Kori gave him her best questioning look.

"Do you know how he got his money?" Zach asked, clearly not ready to tell her why they were there to talk about Larry yet.

Kori shook her head and looked at him. She could tell it wasn't going to be good whatever came out of his mouth.

"We looked into him. Really anyone who had an account with recent activity at Heidi's bank in Scoter Circle was put on their radar. But they had nothing on Larry. He . . . he's not someone you want to associate with."

Kori raised her eyebrows in question. She was happy to hear that Zach was giving information about account holders. She now needed to find out if Wesley had one.

"He was suspected of drug trafficking years ago. Rumor has it that he bought his way out of a conviction and gave up his co-

conspirators in the process. In exchange, he was given his freedom and was allowed to keep his cash, which would have been confiscated with a conviction."

"Wow. In Scoter Circle? I thought that place was as safe as Hermit Cove."

"Yeah. Well. We did have a murder not long ago, you might remember."

They both laughed. Of course she remembered. She'd basically solved it. With Zach's and Nora's help of course. Now she was hoping to do the same with Zach's and Jay's help.

"Okay, so Larry is worth staying away from even if he is guilty because he's dangerous and will get away with it. Point taken. What about Wesley Sanders?" Kori asked, mentally moving down the list.

"Who? I haven't heard that name. In Scoter Circle?"

"No. He's a Wall Street Broker in New York."

"Why is he even on your list?"

Kori poured batter for two large pancakes on the hot griddle and sliced bananas on top of them. "Jay was able to hack into Heidi's online dating profile and they'd recently talked. I don't know the details of their conversation but Jay thought he was worth looking into. And my mom overheard this weekend in Scoter Circle that any recent online boyfriends were suspects."

"Well, I can't help you there."

"And Oscar Baer?" He was the last one on Kori's list.

"Brett's cousin," Zach said. "Heidi talked to him through the dating site?"

Kori nodded. "According to Jay anyway."

"Hmm. I know Scoter Circle Police talked to him but I don't know the outcome of the discussion."

"But you'll find out?" Kori asked hopefully.

"I'll see what I can do."

"Hey, and do you know if Brett has a girlfriend?" Kori thought back to the Barbie in his front yard.

"Yeah. He does. What made you think that?"

"Well . . . I told you I was helping Jay with something yesterday?" Zach nodded and gave her an encouraging look to continue. "We went to Scoter Circle to talk to Brett. And I followed him home— don't worry, he didn't see me—and I saw a real life Barbie greet him. I just thought that maybe Heidi was getting in the middle of that relationship and that was his motive for killing her."

In a very serious tone, Zach warned her, "Kori, I don't want *you* getting in the middle of this investigation and giving someone a reason to kill you. I can't believe that's what you were helping Jay with."

"I know. I should have told you. But don't worry. I'm just helping Jay clear his name."

"You know I can do that, right?"

Kori nodded, suddenly feeling guilty for maybe overstepping her ground with this relationship. She didn't want Zach to think that she was using him for information. Because that was anything but the case. "I know. And you will. I'll just—"

"You'll just not be connected to this at all. I gave you the information I could, but please don't do anything . . . stupid."

"You keep saying that," Kori teased. "You think I'll do something stupid, don't you."

"No. I don't. I just don't want to see you get hurt."

Kori flipped the pancakes. "I'll keep you posted on my sleuthing."

"I guess I'm not going to be able to stop you?" he asked.

"Nope. But I'll let you know if I find anything good."

Zach paused to take a sip of coffee. Kori put Lani's pancakes on a plate and placed it in front of her. Finally, Zach said, "There's been a development since yesterday."

"What kind of development?" Kori asked.

"You said you were in Scoter Circle yesterday?" Kori nodded in answer to his question. "There was another murder. At the conference center."

Kori stopped working and looked up to meet Zach's eyes. She was afraid of what he might say next.

"There was no DNA but the receptionist at the conference center where the murder took place identified Jay's photo as having been there right after it happened."

Kori felt the blood leave her face. How could she have been so stupid? Of course they should have stayed away from any crime scene, even if they hadn't known it was a murder. Jay was already a person of interest, if not a full blown suspect. And there she was, putting her older brother in harm's way by bringing him straight to the town where Heidi had been killed. Of course someone would have recognized him.

And Meri hadn't been very friendly, especially once Kori brought Ibis inside. She felt even worse remembering that mistake. She'd brought attention to them when she should have tried to stay under everyone's radar.

"Okay. But we didn't even know what the crime scene was. All the receptionist told us was that there was a crime scene in the conference center. Why were they even letting people inside?" Kori asked.

"They only blocked off half of the building. And you happened to show up right after it happened."

"You don't think we went there to kill someone, do you? Who was the victim?"

"Larry Downing."

"Oh my God." If Kori had been concerned over where they'd been, she was terrified now. "Do you think Jay's in danger? Do you think I am?"

"I would suggest neither of you goes back to Scoter Circle any time soon if that's what you're asking."

In the lull in conversation as Kori absorbed this new turn of events, the front door opened and Jay walked in with Spencer Graff. They were laughing about something so Kori assumed everything had been smoothed over with Jay suddenly taking yesterday afternoon off. She had no idea what Jay had used as an excuse. She also suddenly remembered his gun. Had he taken it from the glove box when he got out of the car and she just hadn't noticed?

Both men waved and smiled at Kori and took a seat in a window booth. They looked relaxed and Kori decided to keep the new information to herself. Jay was always trying to protect her. Not it was her turn to repay the favor.

Before she could even walk over to take their order, Vera Joy and Betsy Scoop entered the café, followed by two families of out of town visitors. Not only could Kori spot tourists because she didn't recognize them, but also because they looked lost and hesitant to seat themselves. These families followed Vera's and Betsy's lead and found two empty booths.

With the café nearly full to capacity, Zach and Detective Silver finished their breakfast, left cash and waved goodbye to Kori as she made the rounds for orders.

"How's Bella doing in her new home?" Vera asked.

"Bella?" Kori asked, confused.

"The dog. You didn't give her away did you?" Vera's face showed more concern than necessary.

"Oh right! No, of course not. I just changed her name and already forgot that she used to be called Bella. I named her Ibis. After a bird with similar coloring."

"A bird, of course," Betsy joked. "She wouldn't be a Cooke without a bird name."

Kori smiled and took their orders, then moved on to the next booth, slowly working her way to Jay and Spencer.

When she finally made it there, she decided she had to be blunt about Jay's gun without it seeming out of the ordinary to Spencer. She gave it her best shot. "Jay, did you leave anything in my car last night when I dropped you off?" she asked in her best innocent voice.

"No, I don't think so." Ignorance truly was bliss. Jay was still plenty relaxed.

"Good. I just didn't see you take anything but I must have just missed it."

Jay's face suddenly blanched. "Oh my God."

"So you did forget something?" she asked, trying to remain calm. "Because I checked later and I didn't see anything." She realized that this conversation was starting to sound more and more suspicious.

"No, I did forget something. You didn't see it?"

Kori shook her head, starting to reach the same level of panic as Jay.

"I'll stop by later and double check," he said, regaining his composure.

"Great. What can I get you both for breakfast?"

Kori was busy the rest of the morning, making more batches of popovers than anything else, even the omelets which were usually the biggest seller.

At one, Kori flipped the sign around, locked the door and took Ibis outside for another walk. She was thankful that Ibis could spend the whole morning without needing to go out. She wasn't sure what she'd do otherwise.

As she rounded the final corner to go home, she saw her mother standing outside the café. It wasn't part of her routine to show up on Tuesday afternoons so she hoped everything was okay.

"Hi Mom," Kori said, coming up behind her.

"Oh, there you are. And with a dog? When did you get her?"

"Sunday. I forgot to introduce you to her yesterday. This is Ibis."

Gale smiled at the name and bent down to pet her. Ibis sat and let Gale shower her with attention.

"What's up?" Kori finally asked.

"You won't believe it," Gale said, hands waving to emphasize her point. Kori refrained from rolling her eyes. "I just found out that Jay's DNA was at Heidi's murder! I had no idea he knew her! What was he doing there?"

"Why are you asking me about this? Shouldn't you be talking to Jay?" Kori asked, unlocking the door and going inside, Ibis and Gale right behind her.

"Oh you know how he is. He just closed right up when I started asking him about it." Kori could imagine. "So I came to you."

"How'd you find out about the DNA?"

"Well, you know my friend Jan Collins?" Kori nodded. "Well, we were at yoga just now—you should start coming with me—and she went to the Auto Body this morning and over heard Jay and Spencer talking about it. I can't believe you didn't tell me. You knew, didn't you?"

Kori nodded.

"What was he doing in Scoter Circle this weekend?"

"He wasn't there. That's the weirdest part. And it hasn't been confirmed as his DNA. All they know is it's a male relative of mine. I'm in the system because of my arrest for Tessa's murder. But they haven't been able to definitively pin this on Jay."

"And he knew Heidi?" Gale asked, sitting at a booth. Kori took the seat across from her.

"Not well. They met on an online—" She had to cut herself off before she gave away one of Jay's secrets.

"Online? How do you meet someone online?"

Kori shook her head. "I don't know. Maybe she was a friend of a friend or something. But he talked to her a couple years ago and not since. So it doesn't make any sense."

Gale's face turned serious and she was unable to look at Kori. "So they just know it's a male relative of yours whose DNA was there?" Kori nodded and Gale continued. "What about Tyler? Weren't you asking about him?"

"Yeah. That's why. We looked him up on Facebook but we couldn't figure out if there was any connection to Heidi. And he doesn't live around here."

"Well . . ." Gale started and paused. She looked down at her hands on top of the table. Kori waited patiently for her to continue. "I don't know how to tell you this." She paused again. "But there's something you should know about your father."

Kori looked at her mother in shock. Was he still alive? She'd gone to the funeral. Had it all been a ruse to get him out of their lives?

"He was married before we met." Gale paused again.

Realization started to dawn on Kori. "Did he have any kids?" she asked.

Gale nodded, still unable to look Kori in the eye. "One son. I don't know his name. All I know is the mother's name is Sharon. I told your father I didn't want to know anything else. It was all part of his life before me and it didn't matter to me that he had another family."

"How could we not have known his son, our brother?" Kori asked, more angry that her dad had kept a half brother from her than that he might now be a killer.

"His ex-wife didn't want anything to do with him. And your father was fine with not knowing his son. I guess that should have been my first warning sign." Kori couldn't agree more. "But what's done is done. We both know Jay didn't kill Heidi so it must be whoever this other man is."

"Do you know how I could find him?" Kori asked, almost positive that it would be Brett Carr, Larry Downing—who was now dead anyway—or Wesley Sanders. "Where did they live when they were married?"

Gale shook her head. "I don't know. That was all so long ago. I wouldn't even know where to start."

"Why didn't you tell us sooner? I have to call Jay."

"I don't know." Kori was floored by how guilty and ashamed her mother looked. "I didn't mean to keep it from you. But it was part of your father's life, something he should have wanted to tell you.

And then he was gone and you were both grown and it was never the right time."

Kori nodded. She didn't envy being in her mother's position knowing she had a secret she was keeping from her kids.

"So, what about coming to yoga with Jan and me sometime?" Gale asked, changing the subject and perking up at a lighter topic.

"Yeah . . . maybe." Kori was too distracted to really think about it.

"Great. Think it over. I've gotta run. Sorry to drop this bombshell on you."

Kori waved offhandedly and sent Jay a message: *Come now. News about suspects. Going to Heidi's memorial.*

While she waited, she cleaned up the kitchen but couldn't get the news from her mother out of her head. She had another brother. And he had to be the murderer.

CHAPTER 8

As soon as Jay walked into The Early Bird Café Kori blurted out, "We have a half brother. Mom just told me Dad had another family. He was married before they met."

She could see that Jay was trying to make sense of her hurried news without thinking she'd completely lost her marbles and needed to be admitted to a mental institution. She kept talking before he could say anything. "He has to be Heidi's murderer. And maybe even Larry's."

"Wait, what?" Jay sat down, a dazed look still stuck on his face. "Slow down. Start over. We have a brother? Larry's murderer? And let's talk outside so I can check your car for my gun. You really didn't see it?" he asked.

Kori shook her head and walked outside. "I'll start with your first question. Dad was married before he met Mom," she started and explained everything more slowly about not knowing how to find their brother but knowing that finding him would be the missing key to the puzzle.

Jay looked at her in shock, waiting for her to unlock her car. Finally, he said, "What if we just called the bank and pretended to be one of these guys. We'd at least find out if they have an account there. It might narrow it down a little."

Kori was skeptical. She unlocked the car and got in the driver's seat. Jay sat in the passenger's seat and opened the glove box and started rooting around inside it.

"The first thing they'll ask is for the account number. Or the last four digits of your social security number. Or your verbal password. They won't even let on that they know the name until they're sure it's really the account holder on the line, and not someone pretending to be them."

"You're probably right." Jay got out of the front seat and got in the back to keep looking.

Kori turned around in her seat to face him. "But if we can find out which of them is Sharon's son, we might be able to narrow it down and take our chances with one call."

"I'm on it," Jay said, pulling his phone out of his pocket. Kori expected him to get online but instead he started dialing a number.

"Who are you calling?" she asked.

Jay looked at her sheepishly. "The new girl I've been seeing—or, well, talking to. She works in Scoter Circle with the Office of Public Records."

"And you decided not to tell me until now?" Kori was excited for her brother but annoyed that he'd been withholding information that could have helped them clear his name—and find their brother—faster.

"It didn't seem relevant until now." Jay leaned back against the seat and held up one finger as he listened to the person who answered the phone. After a pause, he said into the phone, "Could I please speak with Paula Short?" Kori waited again for Jay to speak when she assumed Paula came onto the other line. "Hi Paula, it's Jay . . . I'm good, how are you? . . . No, I'm actually calling about a family thing . . . I just found out I have a brother I didn't know about and I was hoping he was a resident at some point in Scoter Circle . . . No, I don't know his name. But his mom's name is Sharon . . . He's gotta be about ten years older than me . . . Great. Thanks. Bye."

Kori was surprised that he hung up without getting any information. "What was that about? She can't help?"

"No, she can. She's going to pull records for anyone named Sharon with a son close to the age we think he'd be. She'll call me back."

"Well, in the meantime, let's get going to Scoter Circle for Heidi's memorial. No gun?"

"No gun. I have no idea where it is. Again. And I'm not sure it's the best idea for me to go to the memorial. If I was already recognized in Scoter Circle yesterday I don't think I should be showing my face there again today. Especially at Heidi's memorial."

Kori knew he was probably right. "Fine. Take Ibis with you. I'm going alone then."

Jay nodded, got out of the car and headed back toward the front door to the café.

Kori couldn't believe Jay's gun was really missing. Where could it have gone from the time they left the café, drove to Scoter Circle and she dropped off Jay at home? Could Brett have taken it?

She drove like a madwoman to Scoter Circle, not missing the turn this time. She was a half hour early for the memorial so decided to drive by Brett's house. She was thankful that she'd had the foresight to figure out where he lived.

As she turned down his street, she slowed down and checked her rearview mirror to make sure no one was following her. She knew she had to cover all of her bases if she was going to stay safe. Meri and Brett would likely recognize her, but she didn't think anyone else in Scoter Circle knew her. That was definitely to her advantage.

As she drove by Brett's house, she saw lights on and knew she had to keep going. But she made a mental note to circle back later. He'd likely be at the memorial. Maybe a better plan was to get inside his house and check for Jay's gun.

She also wanted to check out Heidi's house. She pulled over to the side of the road, pulled out her phone and checked the online memorial notice. Thankfully, it listed Heidi's address. And the memorial was about to start, all the way across town. Instead of heading for the memorial, Kori went to Heidi's address.

She parked a block away and calmly walked toward the listed address. The street was empty and Kori figured all of the neighbors were at the memorial. It was probably a close knit, small community and she wouldn't be noticed because no one was home. At least that was what she hoped would be the case.

She walked to the corner and then doubled back, checking again for anyone following her. Then she walked to Heidi's front door and knocked.

There was no answer so she tried the front door. It was locked, so she started walking around the house, checking side doors and any windows. She found the back door unlocked and let herself in.

Kori wanted to see if there was any evidence of Heidi personally knowing any of the men she was investigating. She knew Heidi and Brett had a relationship, and Brett was looking more and more guilty, but what about Larry, Oscar and Wesley? Sure, Larry was dead. But maybe the two murders were connected and finding the connection could solve both.

Kori walked straight into the living room, which was filled with matching furniture and was spotless. She knew enough about Jay that this relationship never would have worked once they met in person and she saw how sloppy he was. She didn't know if he even washed his own laundry or waited until he was dating someone who would do it. Though that could take months between cycles.

There was one photo on the wall that caught her eye—Brett with who she assumed was Heidi and their son. If they weren't together, why did Heidi have a family photo up? Was she trying to hold on to something that wasn't there?

The living room was at one end of the downstairs. The whole floor was mostly open so she walked slowly toward the front of the house, careful to keep out of the way of windows. She walked toward the kitchen and dining areas, still looking at anything on the walls.

The thought suddenly crossed her mind that the house wasn't taped off with police tape, like half of the conference center yesterday. Where had Heidi been killed? And wouldn't her house still be off limits? Well, Kori had technically trespassed to enter it, so she supposed it was off limits.

Kori didn't see anything that caught her attention and she didn't want to disturb anything. The kitchen was just as organized as the living room had been so any movement would easily be noticed.

She made her way upstairs and found two bedrooms, one obviously belonging to a child, and a small office. She started in what she had to assume was Heidi's bedroom and was met by a similar theme as downstairs—matching furniture, everything in its place, not a speck of dust anywhere. She couldn't believe that if the police had searched the house they would have put everything back where it went. She had firsthand experience of what a police search looked like. And The Early Bird Café's kitchen had not been left in order after it was completed.

Finally, Kori walked into the small office. She was almost afraid to enter it as soon as she opened the door. There was a desk with a computer and a chair, a bookshelf and a filing cabinet. But nothing was in the same state of tidiness as the rest of the house.

There were no books on the bookshelf; they were strewn across the whole office, which wasn't a big space. And each filing cabinet drawer was left open, papers clearly out of order as if someone had been in a hurry to find something.

Kori carefully leafed through the papers that were left somewhat intact in the filing cabinet but couldn't figure out what kind of filing system had been used.

Suddenly she realized that it was not quite as bright as it had been when she entered the house and decided she'd maybe reached her limit of safely looking through the house. She wasn't quite satisfied with what she'd found—or not found—but she knew she had to put her safety first.

She closed the office door and quietly walked back downstairs. She let herself out the back door and walked through the neighbor's yard and back on to the street where she found her car waiting for her.

She calmly got back in, thinking about everything she'd seen inside, and drove back home. This time she didn't check behind her to see if anyone was following.

CHAPTER 9

Kori swung by Jay's house to pick up Ibis and tell him what she'd found. Neither of them could figure out what the messed up office had to do with the rest of the puzzle pieces and he still hadn't heard back from Paula so she decided to head home. She was exhausted and after a quick dinner, she fell asleep as soon as her head hit the pillow.

As expected, her alarm woke her up at four and Ibis was still curled next to her. As soon as Kori made a move to get up, Ibis jumped off the bed and headed to the door.

"You already know the routine, don't you?" Kori said to Ibis and chuckled. She might have to start getting up earlier so she could take Ibis for a proper walk.

Once Kori was dressed in jeans and a black t-shirt, she led the way downstairs, through the café and out the front door. Ibis never once pulled on the leash, but it was clear that she thoroughly enjoyed her time outside. Kori thought that maybe a near daily visit to Red Clover Farm so Ibis could play with Milo and Otis would be in order soon.

Back in the kitchen, Kori checked what she had available for breakfast. She didn't like leaving things to the last minute, but her late night hadn't given her a chance to get anything prepared ahead of time.

She pulled out frozen—homemade—blueberry muffins and turned the oven on low to defrost them. She didn't have the energy to get too fancy with her egg breakfasts so decided on fried eggs, hash browns and fruit. She'd have to make each order as it came but she wouldn't have to plan ahead.

There was still a lot of granola and yogurt so she decided to offer that again. And finally, cinnamon French toast. She grabbed three loaves of cinnamon bread from the freezer and started defrosting them in the microwave.

Just after five thirty, with the sign turned to open and a coffee in Kori's hand, Gale walked in before her Wednesday morning spin class.

"Morning, Mom," Kori said, less than thrilled to see her. She was still waking up and didn't think she had the energy to sit through any of Gale's high energy stories.

"Kori, you won't believe this," Gale said, waving her hands around to add to the drama.

"I probably won't," Kori agreed sarcastically.

Gale opened the fridge and helped herself to juice. "That new detective Zach hired—what's her name?"

"Lani Silver."

"Right, Lani. You'll never guess who I saw her with last night."

Kori's stomach twisted into knots. Who else did Lani even know in town other than Zach? Had Kori's fears been right? Was Zach interested in her? Who wouldn't be? She was beautiful.

"Jay!"

"What?" Kori wasn't sure she'd heard right. As far as she knew, Jay online dated women online who he didn't have a chance of running into. "Where?"

"That's right. I stopped at the bar on my way home and she and Jay were awfully close. She was giggling like a schoolgirl." Gale held up her hands in defense.

"Are you sure? Jay told me he's been seeing someone named Paula."

"Well, whoever Paula is better high tail it outa there because he definitely has his eye on Lani."

Kori was shocked. She'd even been to Jay's on her way home. He must have gone out after she stopped by to get Ibis. And he hadn't even said anything to her.

"Well that's . . . great," Kori said hesitantly. *Was it great?*

"I'm off to spin. See you tonight at Red Clover Farm."

Gale waved and hurried back out the front door before her words sank into Kori's consciousness. Gale was going to be at Nora's opening. And Kori was going to be there on a date with Zach. Was she ready to let her mother know about this budding relationship?

Kori didn't have time to dwell on that question as the door opened and Betsy Scoop walked in with Jenna Rhodes. They both waved to Kori and took a booth seat.

"Morning ladies, what can I get you today?" Kori asked, two mugs with their regular coffees already in her hand that she placed in front of them.

"Wow, what service," Jenna gushed. "I'll just have a muffin. I've gotta be quick. I have an early morning with the kiddos today. One mom had an early meeting but I couldn't pass up breakfast out."

"I'll take the French toast," Betsy ordered. "I was thinking of trying to make a French toast ice cream to offer at Scoop's Scoops. What do you think?"

"That sounds great but I don't know anything about making ice cream," Kori admitted.

"I know the kids in my day care would eat that up," Jenna added.

Kori headed back to the kitchen to get their breakfasts ready and the morning rush began. Gale's friend Jan came in with her grandkids on their way to school. The year was coming to a close and the kids' energy and excitement for the summer vacation was evident.

A family of six filled up nearly a third of the café for almost an hour, causing a longer wait time than usual but Kori was happy for the business.

Finally, Kori was able to close the café and call Jay. She had way too many things to ask him about. She wanted to find out if he'd been on an actual date with Lani Silver or if he was just trying to get information from her about this case. And she needed to know what was really going on with Paula. Had she given him any information about Sharon and their half brother? And was he dating two women at the same time? That was not who Jay was at all.

He didn't answer his phone so she decided to clean up and catch up on the office work she'd been putting off all week. Sitting down at her desk, Ibis next to her on the only dog bed she should have bought, Kori couldn't help looking up Wesley, Brett and Larry online. A search for Larry Downing brought up plenty of newspaper articles already published about his death. It was ruled a homicide and detectives had a few suspects in mind. Kori wished she knew who was on that list and if Jay was one of the people they were targeting. If the same DNA was found at his crime scene, she figured it would only be a matter of time before he was arrested. Looking through the articles, she learned that he was not a well-liked man and likely had plenty of enemies.

She also found information about his family—never married, no kids, and both parents deceased. But both parents were listed. *What a lonely life he had*, she thought to herself. With no family, and at most a few friends, he had to have had a lonely existence.

Kori couldn't cross him off as her brother but he moved lower down the list. She'd have to verify that the father listed in the newspaper was his birth father and not a step-father or adoptive parent. And since his mother's name wasn't Sharon, he was looking like a stranger rather than a half brother.

She moved on to Wesley Sanders. She'd bookmarked a few pages with information about him from a previous search and was immediately rewarded with useful information that she'd overlooked. She couldn't believe she'd forgotten all of the clues: Wesley was from Scoter Circle; there was no mention of a father; and he was ten years older than Kori. That would make him only seven years older than Jay, but that was still within the general time period that her dad might have gotten someone else pregnant before meeting their mom.

She called Jay again. As she listened to it ring over and over until voicemail picked up, she unconsciously reached down and patted

Ibis' head. When she realized what she was doing, she was relieved to have her by her side.

Kori heard Jay's recorded voice pick up and she hung up. She wasn't going to leave a message. She needed to tell him her realization in person. So she headed outside, Ibis at her heels, and got in her car.

She drove the short distance to HC Auto Body to find Jay, leaving Ibis in the car, and headed into the office. She found Spencer on the phone and pacing behind his desk. He looked up when she closed the door behind her and he held up one finger for her to wait.

". . . Sure, I'll pass on the message . . . Thanks." Then he hung up and turned back to Kori. "What's going on Kori? Have you seen Jay?" he asked, sitting in the chair behind the desk instead of continuing to pace.

Kori was confused. "I haven't seen him since last night."

"He hasn't been in since lunch. He said he had something he had to help you with and just about ran out of here."

Kori had a good idea of where he might be. She waved her thanks and without saying a word left Spencer's office. She thought she heard him call her back in but she couldn't be sure. She was on a mission and blocked everything else out.

Back in her car, she tried Jay's phone again. She wasn't surprised he didn't pick up. Instead of leaving a voicemail, she put the car in drive and headed toward Scoter Circle. She was confident she'd find him there.

***

Kori had too many questions: Why didn't Jay call her back when he heard from Paula? Did Wesley know about Kori and Jay? Had he set Jay up for revenge at having a present father? Was it all just a coincidence? What did Heidi have to do with it?

That last question was eating away at her and she couldn't let it go. Halfway to Scoter Circle she pulled over to take Ibis for a short walk and she used that opportunity to call Heidi's bank. She wasn't sure she'd get anywhere but she had to give it a try.

A hesitant—and young sounding—voice answered after the first ring. She was immediately thankful for businesses answering their phones, unlike her brother.

"Eastern Credit Union, how can I help you?" Kori pictured a twenty year old working at home for the summer as a teller.

"Hi, I'm calling on behalf of Wesley Sanders—" Before she could finish her lie, she was cut off.

"Hi Marsha," the voice said. "As I'm sure you're aware, Heidi no longer works here and we haven't had a chance to hire her replacement to personally oversee Mr. Sanders' safety deposit box. I know that he likes to know the person overseeing its security, and I can assure you that as soon as we have someone in place we'll let him know."

Kori heard some scuffling in the background and a man's voice came on the line. "Who is this?" he asked gruffly. "Marsha? Is that you?" Then Kori heard him give the phone back to the younger person and speak roughly to her. "Did she tell you her name was Marsha? Did you confirm her identity? We never just assume who it is."

Then the line went dead.

But that answered Kori's most important question: Heidi had been Wesley's personal link at the bank where something important to him must have been kept in a safety deposit box.

Kori got back in her car, Ibis in the back seat, and drove even faster to Scoter Circle, dialing Jay's number half a dozen more times. As she approached the center of town, she started looking around for Jay's car. She didn't know where Paula's office was but hoped it was near downtown. If she'd called Jay—like Kori suspected—then he probably went to her office to get whatever information she'd come up with.

Just as she was crawling toward an intersection, a car came speeding from the road on her right and flew toward the stop sign. Kori hit her brakes just in time, but then the other car suddenly stopped, half in her lane.

Kori continued slowly through the intersection, turning just in time to see the other car start approaching her as she passed. She stepped on the gas and floored it out of the way before she was hit.

Her heart was pounding as she continued driving, glancing in her rearview mirror to see the other car turn right behind her, swerve into the other lane, then overcorrect and drive off the road to the right.

Kori knew she'd missed an accident by just a few inches and she slowed down to see what was happening behind her. Pulling over and stopping, she assumed the other driver was too drunk to be on the road so she dialed 911.

She got out of her car and walked slowly back toward the other car that was still off the road. The driver hadn't yet emerged.

"Nine one one, what's your emergency?" the dispatcher said.

Kori continued toward the car. "Hi. I'm in the center of Scoter Circle and a car just went off the road behind me. I think the driver must have been drunk," she said.

"Is anyone hurt?"

"I don't know. No one was hit. But I can't see the driver."

"I'll have an ambulance on its way."

Kori hung up. She knew she shouldn't have, but she had to make sure the driver was okay without being distracted by the dispatcher asking her questions.

As she got closer to the car, she saw that the driver was moving. She could see that it was a man, older than herself, and that he was trying to open his door.

When he got the door open, she couldn't believe who stepped out of the car.

CHAPTER 10

Kori was only a hundred feet from Wesley Sanders. And he was struggling to stay on his feet. She didn't know if it was from severe intoxication or the accident or both. But he was coming toward her and he had a look of recognition on his face.

Kori stopped in her tracks. His expression was not one of happiness; there was a sneer on his lips.

"If it isn't Kori Cooke," he said, stumbling closer to her.

Kori felt in her pocket for her phone. She suddenly wished she'd let Ibis out of the car. It was still mid afternoon so anyone could see them, but there wasn't much traffic and of the few cars who'd driven past, no one stopped. She hoped the ambulance would be there soon.

"I'm sorry, I'm not sure I know you," she stammered, hoping her voice sounded stronger than she felt.

"Kori Cooke. Don't tell me you don't know me; your own brother. Well, let me introduce myself. Wesley Sanders. I know. You're thinking I should share your last name since we share a father. But he wasn't quite what my mom was looking for in a partner so she gave me her name."

Kori continued to stare at him blankly, keeping her distance. If it was his DNA at Heidi's murder, she wondered how she was going to get a confession out of him. And if it would even matter with no other witnesses around.

"You're not going to just let me stand here without a hug, are you?"

Wesley started coming toward her again and she took a step back. She scanned him up and down, looking for anything that could be a weapon.

"You don't trust me?" he asked, the sneer growing. "I wouldn't hurt my own baby sister."

The words came spilling out of her mouth before she could stop them. "You have no right to take this out on me. Or on Jay. Our father might not have been the best dad but there was nothing either of us could have done to change that."

"Oh, so he wasn't what you were looking for in a dad either?"

Kori regretted telling him that now. She didn't know if or how he'd use it against her. If that was even his intention. But if he had truly done to Heidi what she thought he had—and maybe even to Larry—she didn't want to think about what else he was capable of. She kept her mouth shut again.

Thankfully, she heard a siren approaching and she relaxed just slightly, glancing behind her to see if the ambulance was in sight. It wasn't.

Before she could turn back around to look at Wesley, he had his arm around her neck, her back to his front, and she panicked. She felt the tip of a gun at her back, safely hidden from any passing cars between their two bodies.

He said straight into her ear, "I've waited years for this moment. I've known about you and Jay and Gale all my life. But I used that hatred to fuel my own success. Until Jay got involved with Heidi. That was his downfall."

Wesley paused and Kori let those words sink in. *His downfall? Had he killed Jay? Was that why he wasn't answering his phone?*

Wesley started forcing Kori backwards toward his car off the road. She panicked even more, trying to pry his arm off from around her neck, looking around franticly for the ambulance that she knew would show up soon. She needed it to be soon or she was afraid of what would happen to her.

"You might think I'd want to frame Brett. That would have been perfect, wouldn't it? The history of abuse. A broken household. A son he doesn't care for. But no. I needed something to make me feel better after Heidi made that mistake weeks ago. I never should have trusted her with my safety deposit box."

Kori wasn't sure what he was talking about. *What had Heidi done? What did he have to feel better about? And why did he have to kill Heidi?*

She didn't know how close to his car they were but they continued moving backwards.

"Larry had no business seeing what I was keeping in there. And Heidi knew it. But she couldn't help herself. He was such a smooth talker. That's how he made all his billions—by preying on young women who were financially insecure and taking advantage of the people they knew. But he picked the wrong person to mess with."

What had Wesley been hiding?

"Heidi claimed it was an accident that she opened up my box when Larry came in for his. But she knew both of us personally, if you know what I mean. There was no way it was an innocent mistake. And now my career has been ruined. Those documents were never supposed to be found. I should have just burned them."

Documents? What documents? Was that why Heidi's office at home had been torn apart? Had Wesley broken in to look for those documents?

She pulled at his arm harder and suddenly he released her. She stumbled forward, landing face first on the ground, and then turned around to see Jay standing over Wesley. The trunk was open and Jay was holding a tire iron.

"I don't know what he was thinking. If he killed me, he would have been the only one left to blame for Heidi and Larry's death. Without my DNA, he was doomed," Jay said, calmer than Kori could imagine.

Just then, the ambulance arrived, followed by two police cars.

"I believe this is the man you've been looking for," Kori said, pointing to an unconscious Wesley lying in a heap on the ground. "He's responsible for Heidi Fischer and Larry Downing's deaths. He's my half brother so you can check his DNA for a match."

***

It was hours later that Kori and Jay finally made it back to Hermit Cove. They'd had to wait for Wesley to wake up before he was arrested and they gave their statements. Then they started asking questions to figure out what had really happened. Thankfully, with a call from Zach to convince Scoter Circle Police Department to tell them what happened, their questions were finally answered.

Wesley had been a long time customer of Heidi's bank and had trusted her as soon as he'd met her. He'd almost solely communicated with her through the online dating website to conceal any conversations they had. The documents he'd been hiding in his safety deposit box had contained information about all of the insider trading he'd been doing during his sixteen year career on Wall Street. Heidi hadn't known what it was but Larry had bribed her to let him see what was inside.

Wesley knew that if word got out about his trading habits he'd be ruined. He'd lose everything and spend the rest of his life in prison. So he'd gone after Heidi and Larry.

But in the process he decided that he could also satisfy his need for revenge against his unknown father and the family he'd been abandoned for. It was easy enough to get his hands on Jay's gun since Gale was so scatterbrained and had left it in sight in her car during the yoga retreat.

And Jay had been just as careless when he and Kori showed up in Scoter Circle to talk to Brett. He'd taken it a second time and had it in his hand when Jay knocked him out with the tire iron. The previous night, he'd seen Kori back in Scoter Circle and had followed her back to Hermit Cove where she'd gone straight to Jay's house. He'd used that information at lunch to track down Jay and kidnap him. He was planning to finish his revenge and fully frame Jay when Kori interrupted it.

Wesley's fingerprints and DNA were at both crime scenes and Jay was easily cleared.

Once they were finally satisfied with the information Scoter Circle Police Department had given them, Kori drove Jay home for some much needed rest. She couldn't help herself from asking him, even after the long day they'd endured, about Lani. "We've been in touch for a couple months online. She didn't move here for me," Jay told her. "But it sure is a plus." Kori noticed his larger than normal smile.

"What about Paula?" she asked.

"She never was able to find Wesley's information."

Kori glanced at him. "That's not what I meant. You said you've been seeing her."

"Just online. It's not going to work out. She'll be fine."

After dropping off Jay, Kori headed straight to Zach's for her much anticipated date.

She knocked and waited only a few seconds before he came to the door. "You're empty handed," he teased, a smile softening all of his features and making Kori's knees go weak.

"Long day."

Zach stepped away from the door and led Kori into his kitchen. He already had two beers open and handed one to Kori. "To clearing Jay's name," he said, clinking his bottle against hers.

She smiled and took a sip. "And to justice. Hey, that's what I should have named Ibis."

"No. You should get out of the criminal chasing business and go back to what you do best."

"Oh?" Kori said, raising her eyebrows. "You don't think I'm a good detective? I believe I've been faster than the police in the two crimes I've solved."

"Touché." Zach paused and then asked Kori, "So you really had no idea that you had a brother all this time?"

She shook her head. "And I wish I still didn't know. Then all of this could have been avoided. You know?"

"Yup. You ready to go?"

Kori still had half a beer so they stayed a while longer. Finally, Zach pulled stuffed mushrooms from the fridge and handed them to Kori.

"What's this?" she asked, surprised.

"Our potluck contribution. I knew you weren't going to have time to make anything so I made them."

"You made these?" She was even more surprised.

Zach nodded.

"Maybe we should switch jobs; you can run The Early Bird Café and I'll be a full time detective."

"I wouldn't like that. You'd be putting yourself in danger too often," Zach protested, putting his arm around Kori's shoulders and leading the way outside to his car and a date at Red Clover Farm.

IN THE KITCHEN WITH GINNY GOLD

SMOOTHIES

In 2008, on a cross country cycling trip, the women in our group were told, "You ladies can eat like lumberjacks!" It wasn't until six months ago that I realized I still do eat like a lumberjack. (Never trust a skinny chef, right?)

So I'm always looking for ways to fill up. And smoothies are the perfect way to stay full longer. I love to have half a smoothie for breakfast with cereal or eggs or waffles and I find that I'm less likely to need a snack mid morning.

INGREDIENTS

- ½ cup plain or vanilla yogurt
- 1 banana
- ¼ cup strawberries (frozen)
- ¼ cup blueberries (frozen)
- ¼ cup apple or orange juice

Add everything to a blender, blend until smooth and enjoy!

Optional additions include ½ cup spinach or kale or a scoop of a favorite super food powder found at health food stores, in the health aisle of a grocery store or even online.

ABOUT THE AUTHOR

Ginny Gold lives in the high Rockies and wouldn't trade it for the world. She loves anything outdoors—especially skiing, cycling, and gardening, though living at over 9,000 feet does make for a short growing season. You can also find her volunteering with local nonprofits and schools when she's not cooking up her next cozy mystery for her loyal readers.

BEFORE YOU GO . . .

If you enjoyed this installment of The Early Bird Café Cozy Mystery Series, be sure to join my FREE COZY MYSTERY BOOK CLUB! Be the first to know about new releases, promotions, sales, new recipes, and even be entered to receive advanced reader copies. Join the club here—http://www.ginnygoldbooks.com.

OTHER BOOKS BY GINNY GOLD

<u>Rise and Die</u>

Stay tuned for the third installment of The Early Bird Café Cozy Mystery Series summer 2014

If you enjoyed *Deadly Surprise*, the second of The Early Bird Café Series, check out <u>*Queen of Poison*</u>, the second of the Lily Bloom Cozy Mystery Series—written by my mom!

Business at Lily's Beautiful Blooms Flower Shop is growing like weeds after a rainstorm. And she was asked to do the main flower interpretation for the Arts in Bloom opening at the Misty Valley Museum. Everything seems to be coming up rosy until she sees a sleek red convertible drive into the driveway of her neighbor, Ryan

Steele, the man of her dreams. An even sleeker red head climbs out of the car.

She thought that was all she had to deal with until the founder of the museum drops dead in her arms and another body turns up dead with all the flowers pointing right toward Lily.

With help from her mom, Iris, her sister, Daisy and their friends Marigold and Tamara, Lily lays out the flowers and tries to rearrange them to point to the real killer. Can she sort it out in time before a third body—maybe hers—ends up in the perennial garden? Can she get her romance growing again with the handsome police chief of Misty Valley?

Chapter 1

Lily's phone was ringing nonstop. *I don't have time for this right now.* "Hello Mom. What's the problem?"

Iris blurted out in her usual dramatic fashion, "Someone stole your father."

That got Lily's attention. "What?" This was more intense than Iris usually managed.

"Your father is gone."

"Of course he's gone. Dad died three years ago. Did you just notice this today?" Lily wondered if Iris had overdone it with her medical marijuana again.

"Don't be a smart aleck. Someone stole the urn with his ashes."

Lily picked up her quilted tote covered with a colorful arrangement of flowers and her appointment book. "Meet me at Beautiful Blooms. I'll be there in ten minutes." She hung up before Iris had a chance to say any more nonsense. Lily still missed her father. He had been the mediator between the three Bloom women—Lily, her sister Daisy, and their mom, Iris. He was easy going and had a great sense of humor which always squashed the tension if the women got too testy. Lily had her father to thank for her Beautiful Blooms Flower Shop too. She'd used the money he left her to buy the building and get it started, against her mother's wishes. Iris considered it a boring choice but it had been Lily's dream and the town was wildly supportive of her business.

"Come on Rosie. You can come to work with me today." Rosie wagged her tail and rushed to the door. Lily let them out the back door and walked to her minivan, still thinking about her dad. She was shocked when she looked up and saw a red mustang convertible driving into her neighbor's driveway. *I wonder who is visiting Ryan Steele this early in the day.* A tall red headed woman got out of the car and grabbed a suitcase from the back seat.

Lily realized she had stopped and was gawking at the newcomer. The red head looked up and waved to Lily. "Good morning."

Lily returned the wave and quickly got into her car. Ryan hadn't mentioned anyone coming to visit. Ever since he'd been hired as the permanent police chief of Misty Valley she didn't see much of him. But still, she thought this would have been newsworthy. He never even mentioned that he had a girlfriend which was odd since she thought he was interested in her. *I knew there had to be a catch. Everyone thought he was perfect,* she thought.

Iris's yellow, convertible VW bug was already parked in front of Lily's flower shop. *This day is not starting well.* "Come on Rosie. Let's get this over with." They walked through the front gate and small garden in front of the shop, opening the door to the familiar jingle from her antique bell.

Iris was having an animated conversation with Daisy about the disappearance of the urn. "I never told you girls, but that urn is very valuable. It was handed down from my grandmother to my mother to me. I bet whoever stole it is in for a surprise when they discover it's filled with someone's ashes." Iris laughed at that thought. They turned their attention to Lily when she walked in. "Lily. What should we do about it? Call your handsome cop friend?"

"Call him if you want to. He has a tall red head visiting so he might be busy," Lily said with disdain as she threw her tote and appointment book onto her cluttered desk in the back work room.

Daisy laughed. "What's the matter Lily? I thought you didn't like the handsome Ryan Steele. It sounds like you're a little jealous."

The brass bell above the door jingled again as Tamara Biotchi made her grand entrance. "You won't believe it. Someone broke into my house and stole my grandmother's antique table."

Lily, Iris and Daisy all stopped what they were doing and looked at Tamara. "Stole your table?"

"It was a small table, but very valuable. Who would do a thing like that?"

Iris sounded furious. "Someone stole my husband. What's going on in this town?"

Tamara looked at Iris, full of concern. "Your husband is dead. Are you sure he was stolen?"

The door jingled as Ryan Steele and his beautiful lady friend walked in.

"The urn with his ashes were stolen, you ninny. The urn is valuable. And of course the ashes are priceless to me," she remembered to add.

Ryan looked concerned. "What was stolen?"

Tamara and Iris both started talking about the stolen table and husband, their voices escalating so nothing could be understood.

Ryan held up his hands. "One at a time. Did I hear you say your husband?" Ryan finally got the story straight. "Come to the station and fill out a report. You two aren't the only ones in town to have had something stolen." He turned his attention back to the striking person standing quietly by his side. "This is Jennifer. She's staying with me for a few days. I just wanted to show her around town before I get busy at work."

Lily stormed to the back room without any greeting. Ryan watched her leave and asked Daisy, "What's wrong with your sister this morning? Did she get up on the wrong side of the bed?"

Daisy smirked. "You'll have to ask her, I guess."

"No time now. Come on Jennifer. I'll walk you to the library, then you'll be on your own till lunch." Ryan looked once more toward the back and shook his head mumbling, "I can't figure her out."

Tamara and Iris left for the police station, still discussing the stolen items.

Daisy found Lily standing at the design table, stabbing yellow chrysanthemums into foam for a big funeral piece. "What's your problem Lily? A tad jealous?" She loved needling her big sister about the on-again-off-again attraction Lily had with the handsome, and everyone had thought eligible, Ryan Steele.

Lily kept working furiously. "So he has a gorgeous girlfriend. Big deal. I have other things to think about now."

Daisy laughed. "If you say so."

Lily finally slowed down and looked at Daisy. "Why does he get under my skin so easily?"

"Duh. Because you like him."

"Not today." Lily finished the arrangement and put it in the cooler. "Now I have to get going on the arrangement for the Art in Bloom opening at the museum tonight."

Daisy wrapped a bouquet of roses and baby's breath. "Pretty sweet that you got to do the centerpiece of the show. Who's sitting with us at the reception tonight?"

Lily scowled. "Ryan was supposed to but I don't want him bringing that woman. You, Mom, Tamara, Marigold and Melinda."

"There's room for Jennifer too. You may as well find out who your competition is."

Lily looked at Rosie. "Do you want to come and take that seat?"

Rosie wagged her tail, always up for an outing.

Daisy laughed. "She is a celebrity ever since she caught that murderer and saved your life. Maybe you could sneak her in."

***

The Misty Valley Museum was in an historical building owned by Marion Barry, an eccentric lady with a passion for floral artwork. The brick and clapboard museum was surrounded by a lovely perennial garden on Lupine Lane, just down the street from Lily's Beautiful Blooms Flower Shop.

Lily had her arrangement all set and ready to deliver by mid-afternoon. It had tall royal blue delphinium, green bells of Ireland and orange lilies nested in moss flowing over the sides of a dark blue handmade ceramic dish. She had an antique mirror to place it on, giving the effect of an island garden on a pond. "What do you think Daisy?"

Daisy's hand went over her heart. "It's stunning Lily. Those colors and the reflection are absolutely beautiful. Do you need help moving it to the museum?"

Lily looked around the shop. "It's pretty quiet. Let's lock the front door so you can come too. We can get a quick preview of the other arrangements while we're there."

Lily carefully placed the arrangement in her van and they drove the half mile to the museum.

Elizabeth Stevens, the museum director, was greeting everyone as they delivered the various flower displays for the Art in Bloom opening. It was an annual event where anyone could pick a painting and interpret it with flowers. The museum had been sponsoring the event for several years and it was very popular.

She fluttered her hands when she saw Lily. "I knew you would make a magnificent arrangement. Follow me. I have a table all set up for you right inside the entryway." Elizabeth's high heels clattered on the slate tiles. "Everyone will see your flowers as soon as they walk in. Marion insisted that her favorite floral painting would be the centerpiece this year. Put it here. Right next to the painting."

Lily carefully put the mirror and flowers on the small table next to the painting. They all stood back. Elizabeth gasped. "I hope Ms. Barry isn't upset if her painting gets upstaged by your flowers. I've never seen a more striking arrangement."

Lily blushed slightly from all the compliments. "Thank you, Elizabeth. Do you mind if Daisy and I take a quick peek at the other arrangements?"

Elizabeth patted Lily's shoulder. "Go right ahead. This is my favorite time of year. The Art in Bloom show brings so many more people into our special museum than any other art show we have. You will be back tonight for the reception I hope."

Lily nodded. "Of course. I have a table full of friends and family."

Elizabeth clapped her hands together. "That's great. Ms. Barry is speaking tonight at the dinner. She hasn't always felt well enough to attend for the last few years. She's excited about her new painting and since her niece and nephew are coming, she didn't want to miss this year. I'll be sure to introduce you."

Lily and Daisy started to walk away but Elizabeth stopped them, looking concerned. "Have you heard about the recent antique thefts happening around town?"

Lily was surprised word had spread so fast. "What have you heard?"

"Tamara Biotchi had an antique table stolen and several other people had antiques taken from their homes." She lowered her voice to a whisper. "I have extra security here at the museum. I don't think many people know just how valuable these paintings are."

Lily looked around. "I'm sure you are very busy. We'll take a quick look around and see you tonight at the reception."

"Thank you, Lily. Your arrangement is perfect. See you tonight." Elizabeth turned her attention to another person coming with an arrangement, oohing and aahing over their flowers.

Lily and Daisy giggled as they made their way up the grand staircase to the upstairs galleries. "She's wound tighter than an antique clock. Hope she doesn't have high blood pressure. This extra stress won't do her any good."

Daisy stopped at the top of the stairs in front of a portrait of Marion Barry. "She looks like a dour old lady. This flower arrangement of dark blue monkshood with a white calla and one red rose does capture the mood of the painting quite well. Don't you think?"

"And the black cloth over the table with a pair of old metal frame glasses creates a somber image for sure. It will be interesting to meet her. She never married and has always been a bit of a recluse. I wonder who will inherit all her wealth."

Daisy and Lily stood shoulder to shoulder looking at the painting and flowers. "I hope the monkshood isn't some type of foreboding that a deadly foe is near." Lily shook that thought away and headed back down the stairs. "Let's get back to the shop and clean up so we have time to get ready for the opening tonight."

Chapter 2

Daisy was overloaded with an armful of fancy dresses as she walked into Lily's house. They had a tradition of helping each other decide on what looked best. Daisy loved to get dressed up but Lily preferred to dress casually most of the time. Typically, it was Daisy helping her older sister. It had been like this their whole life.

They pranced around in their underwear, holding up dresses and looking in the full length mirror. Lily grabbed an emerald green slinky, silky dress with a floral design going from one shoulder to the waist. Daisy tried to steal it back. "That's my favorite dress."

Lily swung it away from Daisy's fingers. "Ha. I got it first. I want to look extra special tonight."

Daisy pulled a red flowery silk dress from the pile. "Why is that?"

"Just because." Lily slipped the green fabric over her head. It shimmered down her lean body. She twirled and felt the sensuous fabric tickle her thighs. "What do you think?"

Daisy paused to look intently at Lily. "I think you want to look nice for Ryan Steele. Get him away from that red head." Laughing, she added, "Maybe you shouldn't have been so standoffish in the past. He got sick of waiting for you to make up your mind."

Lily angrily denied that accusation. "I don't care about Mr. Steele. I want to look nice since my arrangement is the centerpiece of the show. I need to look my best in case Nina Baldwin is there to take photos and write an article."

"If you say so," Daisy said mockingly.

A knock on the back door startled Lily. "I wonder who that is. Mom is picking us up but she wouldn't bother to knock." Lily went to the door feeling festive and happy.

Ryan Steele was standing outside looking drop dead good-looking, waiting as if she was supposed to be expecting him. Lily was speechless.

He slowly scanned her from naked toes to blond ponytail and whistled his approval. "Wow. You look incredible." He grinned. "You might want to put some shoes on though. I told you I would give you a ride. Don't you remember?"

Lily fidgeted and blushed. "Oh. I made other plans since you have a friend visiting."

"Jennifer?" Ryan chuckled. "My sister? Is that why you've been avoiding me?"

Lily felt her face get hotter and hotter. She stuttered and stammered, feeling like a complete fool, which was how Ryan Steele usually made her feel. "Iris is picking us up. I'll meet you there?" was all she could manage to say in a somewhat strangled voice.

Ryan leaned close to Lily's ear. "You look absolutely beautiful. You should dress up more often." He straightened back up and winked. "See you there. Oh, and by the way, try not to get your dress caught in the door when you slam it. I'd hate for someone else to have to rescue you."

Lily watched him walk to his car. He was never going to let her forget their first encounter when she so clumsily slammed her car door catching her skirt and making her trip and fall. His scent lingered and she silently gave herself a good kick for jumping to the wrong conclusion about Jennifer.

Daisy tapped her arm. "What just happened? Was that Ryan?"

Iris drove in honking which saved Lily from having to make an explanation to Daisy. They piled into the back of her VW bug and headed to the museum. Marigold Harris was in the passenger seat, happily looking around as though she could actually see what was out the window. Being blind didn't slow her down at all.

It was a short half mile drive to the Misty Valley Museum. The street was lined with cars and people were making their way into the main entrance. Iris swerved her bug into a parking spot between two big SUVs, almost taking off her front fender. "How's that for maneuvering?"

Marigold responded with two thumbs up. "I didn't hear any metal crunching so it's fine by me."

Iris helped Marigold out of the car, holding her left arm and giving a running commentary about what was happening. Marigold had her white cane in her right hand tapping along the sidewalk. Daisy and Lily walked behind.

"Wait up you guys." Lily turned around to see Melinda Biotchi and Jack Weaver hurrying to catch up. "Can we sit with you?"

"Of course." Lily asked Jack, "How is it going at the greenhouse?"

Jack looked content. "I couldn't be happier. It's much better than working at the Misty Valley Country Club." He looked at Melinda. "I think Tamara is even starting to like me."

Lily laughed. "Wonders will never cease."

They entered the museum and were greeted by Elizabeth Stevens who was standing next to Lily's arrangement and the floral painting. "Hello. Hello." She leaned toward Lily and whispered, "Everyone loves your flowers. How daring to put blue and orange together, and the mirror makes the flowers and the painting sparkle from the lighting. Ms. Barry is extremely pleased with how the whole show is looking. She's looking forward to meeting you."

Lily beamed. "Thank you. I'm curious to meet her, too."

"I'll find you when she has a moment. Oh, and Nina Baldwin will be taking photos. Be sure to have her get one of you next to your flowers."

Lily glanced at Daisy to see if she heard that exchange. Daisy nodded slightly. Iris and Marigold were already ahead so Daisy pulled Lily away from Elizabeth and they hurried to catch up.

Iris was describing the paintings to Marigold and letting Marigold guess what flowers were used in the arrangement based on the scent. She did an excellent job figuring it all out and seemed to enjoy it more than Iris even though she couldn't see anything. Lily smiled as she watched the two older women. Iris was so content ever since Marigold moved in with her. It gave Iris a focus away from her two daughters, which was good for all of them. And Marigold was thrilled to be out of the nursing home.

The museum was stunning with all the flowers. A trio of violin, cello and piano played classical music at the side of the main staircase. The mixture of flowers perfumed the rooms. All in all, it was perfect.

Lily felt a gentle touch on her arm. Elizabeth was pulling her away from her family and pointing toward an elderly woman standing off to the side. She whispered, "Ms. Barry is free and wants to meet you now."

Lily was surprised to see how tall and straight Marion Barry was. She looked elegant in her black dress with a dark red shawl draped around her shoulders. Her silvery gray hair was cut stylishly just below her chin. She smiled warmly as Elizabeth escorted Lily over and introduced them. She was much warmer in person than how the artist captured her in her portrait.

Ms. Barry extended her hand to Lily. "I'm so glad to meet you Ms. Bloom. I've heard a lot about you from Elizabeth and she was absolutely right when she said you would put together an arrangement to complement my newest painting. And it's wonderful that Misty Valley finally has a flower shop. If you ever need anything, let me know."

Lily was having trouble finding a reply to this generous offer. Suddenly the lights went out. Several seconds of silence were broken by screaming and scuffling. Lily felt a weight fall against her chest. She held on, confused about what was happening. Crashing sounded from the main entryway.

What felt like forever actually only lasted for a few minutes before the lights were back on. Lily saw that she was holding Marion Barry. Iris and Daisy appeared at her side. They both looked wild eyed. "What just happened?"

Lily gently lowered Marion onto an antique Queen Anne chair nearby. "I have no idea but we need to get help for Ms. Barry. Call 911. Is Ryan here yet?" She looked around frantically but couldn't see him through all the chaos.

Elizabeth hovered, wringing her hands and sobbing. "Oh dear. Oh dear. Is she alright?"

Lily looked at Elizabeth and shook her head as she felt for a pulse on Marion Barry's wrist. She felt like she was going to faint. "I think she's dead."

To keep reading, <u>purchase *Queen of Poison* today!</u>

15953395R00079

Made in the USA
Middletown, DE
01 December 2014